# Billy Boy

by

## Thomas J. Hubschman

Savvy Press

Billy Boy

©2001 Thomas J. Hubschman

Published by:

Savvy Press
473 17th St. #6
Brooklyn, NY 11215-6226
http://www.savvypress.com


ISBN: 0-9669877-3-X
LCCN:  2001117330


Printed in the United States of America

# CHAPTER ONE

The Off Track Betting parlor on the corner of Brooklyn's 12th Street and 5th Avenue didn't attract many local shoppers. But it had its loyal contingent of pensioners, laid-off truck drivers and a small but active fellowship that convened there for something other than the action at Belmont and Hialeah.

The OTB especially came in handy for Billy Conover when he wanted to cop an ounce of pot or a handful of Black Beauties. This morning he had a hangover which only a mega-dose of ups could cure. Coffee did little more than make him mobile, and his mother's carping merely drove him out of the house in search of relief.

"Tito around?" he asked a methadone junkie who had been a dope fiend when Billy was still sucking his thumb. Fat now and permanently stoned on the legal dose he picked up at his clinic, chased down with a pint of cheap wine, the meth-head held court at the OTB like a veteran warrior, one of few survivors of a generation decimated by overdoses, gunshot wounds and AIDS.

"Try Manny's."

Billy noted with satisfaction the quiver of apprehension in the man's eyes. He had been causing that reaction ever since people realized he was crazy enough to do anything. "Hey, Billy, jump off the roof!" And he would do it, usually landing on his feet but sometimes not, it seemed to make little difference to him. The other kids had made fun of his recklessness, but over the years his willingness to take any dare—"Swallow this pill, Billy" "I bet you can't drink a whole quart of booze"—gained him a useful reputation. If your enemies thought you were crazy they left you alone. He had had few fights in his twenty-three years, and those were mostly of his own choosing.

Fifth Avenue was awash in sunlight. Having little in common with its namesake in Manhattan, no Tiffany's or Brentano's, no Sachs or Lord & Taylor, it was a shopper's avenue nonetheless, albeit one of discount clothing stores, cheap furniture outlets and mom-and-pop luncheonettes. For better-quality merchandise, locals shopped the malls in Jersey and Long Island where they could find bedroom sets that didn't fall apart before the last payment was made and suits and dresses they could wear to a wake or wedding without anyone snickering behind their backs. Everyone else, especially those getting by on a laborer's or welfare check, had to make do with whatever the discount stores had to offer. When Billy's father was alive, before the blacks took over downtown Brooklyn, his mother did her shopping at A&S and Martin's. Now, thanks to a heart condition, she was lucky to get down to Fifth Avenue a couple times a year to pick up a new pair of slippers or drainboard for the kitchen sink.

Manny lived on Fourth Avenue, the major traffic artery through that part of Brooklyn. The only stores there were auto-parts outlets and bodegas. The tenements above them were occupied by Puerto Ricans, Dominicans and other Latinos. Billy had been to Manny's before, had even made it with Manny's sister on one of the family's sweet-and-sour-smelling cots. That was more than a year ago, and although the girl who was only fourteen at the time promised not to tell, he was concerned what Manny's reaction might be if she hadn't kept her word.

A note scribbled in magic marker on the mailboxes indicated the bells were out of order. The main entrance door was ajar. He pushed it open and entered a dark hallway smelling of last night's rice and beans and the morning Bustelo. Dark halls were hangouts for junkies and other ne'er-do-wells, but this one looked empty, so he headed up the gloomy stairway.

The climb made his head throb more insistently. His evening had started out innocently enough, a few beers on the sidewalk outside Scully's, the major social institution in his neighborhood, not excepting the busy church two blocks away. He was a rare visitor to either anymore, unwelcome at the bar because of his bent for provoking dissension just for the fun of it, and he hadn't seen the inside of Holy Family since Father Tim was curate back during Billy's brief career as a Boy Scout.

When his money had run out and nobody in Scully's was willing to stand him to another quart container, he decided to take matters into his own hands at the twenty-four-hour grocery across the street. The store was run by Pakistanis—a dry cleaner had stood there until the neighborhood began gentrifying a few years back—and they kept a sharp eye out for thieves. But after midnight there was only one man on duty, the theory being no one would try to rob the place with Scully's right across the street. The theory was sound except it didn't account for people like Billy whose skills as a shoplifter were mediocre but whose nerve made up for any lack of talent. After sending the clerk off to find a box of extra-strength tampons, he filled the inside of his jacket with cans of beer and walked out of the store. By the time the clerk realized what had happened, Billy was three blocks away and already consuming his ill-gotten gains.

Later in the evening he returned to Scully's and found a couple old schoolmates willing to buy him a quart just to keep him quiet. He drained it on the sidewalk in full view of the grocery he had robbed earlier. When the clerk spotted him and then began cursing him in vigorous Urdu, Billy waved back cheerfully and called out that he didn't need the tampons after all, it had been a false alarm.

The stairs creaked irritably under his year-old sneakers. This was actually a more solid building than the one in which the Conovers lived, had lived for Billy's entire life. But the mere fact it was inhabited by Latinos, smelled of their cooking and other alien habits, made him feel like he was in a slum. There were no Spanish surnames on the broken mailbox in his own building on 16th Street, and just one Italian. The other tenants were old-time Irish or new people—musicians, office workers—doubling and tripling up in the rundown railroad floor-throughs. The new people came and went, paying top dollar for the same apartment Billy and his mother and sister lived in at a fraction of their rent. The dirty oilcloth was peeling off the crooked stairway and the Conover apartment hadn't been painted for more than a decade. But it never occurred to him that he lived in the same conditions as these Puerto Ricans and Dominicans, for the simple reason he was white and they were not.

He knocked gently at a door on the top floor, waited a few seconds and knocked again harder. There was no radio playing—a sure sign someone was home. He knocked again, then pounded with his fist until the door shook. He could easily have kicked it in, but if he was right about somebody being home they might not take kindly to a stranger busting down their front door, especially if they had a gun.

"Shit," he said loud enough to be heard through the thin wood. His head felt even worse than it had earlier. Even more important, he was slipping into the deep gloom that had stalked him ever since he was a kid. It had been to keep that dark cloud at bay that he set off on last night's drinking bout. Now only ups would dispel it.

He started back down the stairs. The only option left him was to return to the OTB and try to cop off one of the regulars who were usually unwilling to deal to him. Lost to these concerns, he didn't notice the three young men heading up the stairs until he had come face-to-face with them on the second landing. They eyed him with the cautious looks of predators sizing up a tasty but possibly dangerous prey. He suppressed an urge to simply push his way past them. Then a better idea occurred.

"Up against the wall!"

He grabbed the first, a thin Latino, and spun him around against the peeling plaster.

"Now! Or I blow your heads off."

The other two didn't hesitate.

He frisked them quickly, found three switchblade knives and some loose joints, then edged toward the stairs.

"I see you fuckers on my beat again, I haul your asses down the precinct. You got that?"

Three heads nodded reluctantly. By the time they dared look around, Billy was half a block away.

Rosemary Grady, known to her various paramours and clients as Rosy-O, Sweet Rosy O'Grady and Rosy O'Blowjob, was on the phone to her former classmate Cathy Conover. Her older child was taking a bath in the old tub you could only reach by walking out onto the top-floor landing of the brownstone where she lived. The baby was snoring in a Port-a-Crib nearby.

"Danny Matthews says he saw Jinny just half an hour before it happened," she said, her voice hoarse from crying. "He says she looked a little high, but not that bad. Not, you know, like she was gonna O-D or anything. I talked to her mom this morning. She says Jinny had a heart condition. A murmur or something. I never heard nothing like that, did you? I mean, everybody knows Jinny was using crack. Even *I* knew it, and I hardly get out of the house anymore."

Cathleen replied that Jinny's death was such a shock she didn't know what to think yet. But in reality she was only surprised her childhood friend had survived as long as she did. Jinny started using drugs in seventh grade. By the time she was fifteen she was turning tricks on Bartel Pritchard Square just two blocks from her home. By then Cathleen was a sophomore at St. Saviour and had more friends in upscale Park Slope than she did in her own neighborhood. But she wasn't going to risk Rosy's ire by telling her Jinny McCormick only got what she had so long been asking for. In a few years Cathleen would be free of 16th Street, just as soon as she could afford a share in a Manhattan apartment and still have a few dollars left over to give to her mother. Till then, though, she had to pretend she was still one of the girls.

"The wake's tonight," Rosemary said, more than a trace of apprehension in her voice. Wakes weren't her favorite social activity, at least not when the corpse was a close contemporary whose life style didn't differ much from her own. "Ain't that kind of quick? I mean, since she only died last night? But I guess we gotta go."

Cathleen pictured the scene at Roche's Funeral Parlor: half a dozen weepy friends, themselves just a pipe or two from sharing Jinny's fate; the usual pack of red-eyed aunts, uncles and cousins who were no more surprised by how Jinny's life had ended than Cathleen herself was. But she had to make an appearance, even if it meant pretending she wasn't revolted by all those half-stoned unwed mothers and ex-juvenile delinquents.

She got rid of Rosemary and took a quick look at the roasting chicken she had started for her mother. Mrs. Conover suffered from angina, which was why the apartment looked the way it did despite her daughter's attempts to maintain some kind of order. A large living room at the front of the apartment doubled as her brother Billy's bedroom. Cathleen's own small room was located off a long narrow corridor which opened into a dining area. Her mother had set up a narrow cot for herself on the other side of the heavy, dark dining table which hadn't been used since Jack Conover died several years earlier. The kitchen looked out on the gray backs of the buildings on 15th Street. Every other building on 16th Street, a dozen or more tenements, was laid out the same way. When she was a little girl spending most of her time at home or in one of her friend's apartments, Cathleen assumed everyone lived in a similar arrangement.

There was no time to wait for the chicken. She hurriedly changed out of her work clothes and into the black dress she had bought three years ago for an uncle's funeral but which had come in handy several times since.

"You're off to the wake then?" her mother asked. An interior window that helped provide some ventilation on hot summer nights connected the two women's sleeping areas and was left permanently open. After the lights were out it encouraged mother-daughter conversations, which could seem difficult under the glare of a lamp.

"I'll be back in half an hour. The bird'll be done at quarter-to."

"Tell Jinny's mother I'm sorry for her trouble."

"I will," Cathleen said, pulling at the zipper of her dress. Narrowly built, she was a trim size six, with a small waist and long perfect legs, the only obvious legacy from her mother's side of the family. The Donovans were big-bone, wide-hip people, but their women had the finest calves in Brooklyn.

"Your brother might turn up at Roche's himself. See that he comes home with you."

"I'll try."

"Do better than try. He was out all night again. I'm afraid he's in with a bad crowd."

"Billy's twenty-three years old," Cathleen said, trying to free the zipper from a snag. There was no use asking her mother to help. Apart from the angina, which kept her flat on her back most of the day, the woman was also nearsighted but too vain to wear glasses. "If you didn't baby him so much we'd all be better off. Whatever happened to the job Uncle Pat was supposed to find him?"

"Your Uncle Pat talks big, but it's mostly hot air."

"Maybe that's where Billy got it from," Cathleen said, finally yanking the zipper free.

"The boy tries. He really does, Cath-a-leen. There's just no jobs to be had. Look at the newspapers."

"It would help if he went back to school and got his diploma."

"He went down to John Jay just the other day. They told him he has to wait now for the next semester."

"I'll believe it when I see it."

Cathleen emerged from the bedroom, where there was scarcely enough room for her twin bed and a chest of drawers, and presented herself for her mother's inspection.

"How do I look?"

She did not ask from vanity but merely to find out if she had gotten her clothes on straight. But her mother was amazed as always by her daughter's beauty. Try as she might, she could find little resemblance between the girl and herself. Yet she felt no resentment on that account. Her husband had not lived long enough to become a source of bitterness to her, as had the spouses of so many of her friends. She was grateful for this living remembrance of the man who, she acknowledged even when he was alive, was a better-looking man than she was a woman.

"Swell. "

"Then, I'm off. Don't forget the chicken."

"I won't."

"You took your medicine?"

"I did. I'm all set till bedtime."

Cathleen started down the long corridor, then did an abrupt about-face and deftly squeezed around the old Victorian table to give her mother a kiss.

"See you later, love."

By seven o'clock there was already a group of Jinny's friends gathered outside the funeral parlor, conveniently located across the street from the parish church. Patty Brodigan had showed up in a black miniskirt and tights that she sometimes wore to Manhattan discos. Mary Dempsey did Patty one better by wearing black peddle-pushers, a first for Roche's. The funeral director and his granddaughter, a slim attractive blonde who graduated Holy Family Elementary a couple years ahead of Jinny, watched from inside the glass entrance door. Celia Roche had handled this type of funeral often enough to know what the course of the evening would be like: for the first half-hour the immediate family would have the deceased to themselves. Then uncles, aunts and cousins would start to arrive. Finally the dead girl's friends would work up the courage to come inside, approach the viewing room nervously and at the first sight of the coffin all burst into tears. They were a nuisance because they disturbed the other rooms, though it was a rare night anymore that Roche's had more than one body on view, much of the business having gone to the suburbs.

By the time Cathleen arrived, the sidewalk mourners had moved inside and were weeping quietly at the back of the room. The McCormicks were seated in the two front rows on metal folding chairs, whispering among themselves like wedding guests waiting for the bride to arrive. Jinny herself, what was left of her after she had been gutted and stuffed with excelsior, lay in her coffin, her lips looking redder than they should, her already full eyebrows heavily penciled over, making her seem as if she were pondering some question—how many Tuinols she had popped before her last jolt of crack.

Cathleen approached the casket and knelt down on the cushioned kneeler. But as she began her Hail Mary she found that what at first had seemed an authentic if badly made-up version of her childhood friend, up close was clearly a fraud. The rougey woman in the coffin was not Jinny but a chimera conjured up by the mortician's art. The real Jinny had looked a good ten years older, and a hard ten years at that.

She fixed her eyes on the portrait of Christ at the back of the bier and kept them there until her prayer was over.

"I'm very sorry, Mrs. McCormick," she said, taking the hand of a stout, black-draped woman who used to offer her milk and cookies when Jinny and she were in kindergarten. Mrs. McCormick nodded her appreciation without raising her reddened eyes, her two good teeth gnawing her bottom lip as if grief could be masticated like a tough piece of meat. Cathleen went down the line, recognizing all the faces, if not every name—father, brothers, younger sister, even aunts and cousins.

When she reached the last family member, her obligation was formally fulfilled. But custom required she spend some time keeping watch with them. She could park herself on a hard metal chair and kill half an hour chatting with one of the deceased's gabby aunts. Or she could join her contemporaries sobbing quietly at the back of the room. Neither alternative appealed. She was not in a mood for pretending Jinny's death was an act of God, and she had little in common with her old classmates since their paths had divided several years earlier. Even so, she couldn't sit by herself. That would only encourage the notion she was someone who thought herself above them. She decided on two former Girl Scouts standing apart from the others, little lace handkerchiefs pressed to their faces.

"She was so young and pretty!" one of them, a tall skinny girl who used to live on Milky Ways, greeted Cathleen as their cheeks brushed. Cathleen glanced back at the coffin and recalled the sunny pig-tailed Jinny who used to play tag with her in the schoolyard. When you saw someone a couple times a week, if only to say hello to, you didn't notice the minor erosions that were draining vitality from flesh, the consequence of too many crack vials and barbiturates, not to mention the quickies in parked cars to raise money for the next high. Suddenly she found she too was crying. Whatever these young women had become, they were once full of hope like herself, and but for the grace of God she could have shared their fate.

But the mood of moist reconciliation was suddenly broken by a disturbance outside in the reception area. A moment later her brother Billy made his appearance in tattered jeans and dirty denim jacket, his hair scarcely combed, and at least a day's growth of beard. Even from a distance, his eyes seemed unnaturally bright, with a familiar pinwheel look. At first, Cathleen tried to continue her conversation. But the ex-Girl Scout, like everyone else, was waiting to see what would happen next. Billy was impossible when he was high, sometimes impossibly sweet, but more often just plain impossible.

He stood for a moment, not quite steady, thanks to the quart of beer he had used to wash down some pills. He seemed not to recognize anyone, and for a brief moment, his sister dared hope he might simply walk out again. But then he sniffed hard, hunched his shoulders and lurched toward the open coffin.

Despite his disheveled state, she could not help but note the good-looking young man underneath the dirt and drugs. Handsome was too mild a word. He had been a beautiful little boy and had become a beautiful young man, though God knew you had to look hard to see it when he was in the condition he was in tonight. She didn't understand how he could look like that and live the kind of life he did. Not just Jinny, but half the people she grew up with had become dissipated by the time they reached their twenty-first birthdays. Yet, Billy seemed to thrive. And he had the personality to charm the pants off virtually every woman he met and get around most of the men as well. Between his blarney and his looks, he could have gone far. Instead, he chose to become the social pariah she was looking at.

He hit the kneeler in front of the coffin with a thud. Then he stared intently at the face of the corpse as if expecting to begin a dialogue with it. Everyone watched the two dissolutes, one dead, the other still breathing, confront each other. Would he break down and cry? Would he try to embrace the corpse? But after a few moments he merely rose, took a shaky step backward, and, as if with a great act of will, focused on the line of black-draped McCormicks.

He started with the hefty alcoholic brother and worked his way down the row until he reached the diminutive grandmother, solemnly shaking each's hand and offering an inebriate word of sympathy.

When he was done with the family he turned toward the other mourners, spotted a familiar face at the back of the room and stumbled toward her.

"Rosemary!"

Rosemary Grady had arrived just as Billy finished visiting the bier. She had prepared for the occasion by downing a couple shots of Jack Daniels but hadn't worked up the nerve yet to approach the coffin.

"Rosy, I'm sorry about last night," he said loud enough to be heard at the reception desk. "I meant to come by, I really did, but I forgot I had a previous engagement."

"That's okay, Billy," Rosemary said, trying to ease away from her sometimes lover. She actually hadn't seen him in a couple weeks and, as far as she could remember, hadn't made any date with him for last night.

"You know I'd never stand you up like that if it wasn't something important," he went on, putting his hand on her shoulder, as much to steady himself as to emphasize his point.

"Sure, Billy. But you gotta excuse me now. I need to pay my respects, you know?"

"Rosy, you're a sweet girl," he said, still not letting her by. "And you still give the best goddamn head in all of Brooklyn."

Everyone heard. Only the oldest old woman did not know what he meant, and no one was eager to satisfy her urgent inquiries.

Rosemary began to weep with humiliation. But Billy mistook her tears for grief and decided to console her with a beery embrace.

Jinny's oldest brother Mick gently raised his great bulk off his chair in front of the bier and quietly padded toward the back of the room, his face as blank as if he had nothing more on his mind than the men's room. But when he reached the doorway he paused and, without saying a word, slapped his great paw on Billy's neck. Then he gently turned him around and planted his fist in his face.

A gush of bright blood spurted from Billy's nose. He staggered back to the wall where, with its help, he was able to stay on his feet.

"Get the fuck outta here," Mick hissed at him, panting hard. He poked a blunt thick finger into Billy's chest and added, "Next time I see you, you wish you was dead."

Billy was tending to his bleeding nose but found time to reply, "Sure, Mick, sure," as if the will of Mickey McCormick were all he ever considered.

Rosemary stepped forward and began attending to his injury as if he had sustained it defending, not impugning, her honor. But her gesture seemed to infuriate Mick all over again—he was a regular visitor to her "blowatorium," Billy's epithet for her apartment on 16th Street, but was unaware that so were half the other young males in the neighborhood.

Billy seemed to be paying no attention to the freshly erupting McCormick. But just as everyone was anticipating another, possibly lethal blow, he abruptly jammed his hand into the bigger man's midsection and brought his knee up smartly into his groin.

Mick collapsed into a great ball of pain, unable to breathe, much less speak.

The mourners regarded the helpless giant writhing on Roche's tasteful gray carpet, then looked up to see what Crazy Billy would do next. But they found that, like Jesus amongst the hostile Pharisees, he had disappeared from their midst.

# CHAPTER TWO

When Billy left Roche's he headed for Brendan McCauley's apartment on 16th Street. Brendan and he had strung beads together in Miss Shapiro's kindergarten, where she once caught them trying to get Hilda Weisman to show them her nipples. In third grade they helped drive Mr. Fanazio to early retirement and brought Miss Johnson to the brink of a nervous breakdown when she arrived one morning to find her frogs cut into pieces and the class rabbit's back legs missing.

Later they attended Bishop Dodge High School just across the Prospect Expressway. In those days, their favorite hangout was Green Wood Cemetery, a huge park-like piece of land, which abutted the school's back door. The cemetery was a refuge for teenage lovers and other absconders from justice. One weekend a Jewish boy from Borough Park, the cemetery's southern perimeter, and an Irish-Catholic girl from Park Terrace executed a suicide pact there. They were found comatose among the gravestones, intentional overdoses. The boy pulled through, the girl didn't. Billy's class happened to be studying *Romeo and Juliet* at the time, but the young priest teaching the course was reluctant to allow any connection between the day's lurid headline and the offspring of the Montagues and Capulets. Suicide was a mortal sin.

When Billy insisted on the comparison, the priest told him to save the discussion for religion class. Billy told the priest he was an asshole. The priest sent him down to the principal's office, an easygoing duffer just a few months away from an eternal golf game at the diocesan retirement home. The principal spoke gently but backed up the younger priest and suggested Billy's choice of words was excessive. Billy told him he was an asshole too.

Brendan's reason for expulsion was more serious. He was caught walking out of the school after hours with a TV under his arm. When challenged by the school guard, he hit the man in the face with the TV, breaking his jaw.

Brendan quickly learned a more efficient and less risky way of removing people's property from their homes and businesses. He made a few slip-ups along the way, but the time he spent on Riker's Island only honed his skills so that after each release he was able to practice his craft with less liability. What he learned he passed on to Billy, who was a far more willing pupil for Brendan than he had been for Father Gaffney. Brendan's forte was planning and direction, Billy's execution, especially when the assignment required derring-do. He delighted in scaling the backs of buildings which neither Bell Telephone nor the Fire Department willingly took on. He especially enjoyed sneaking into bedrooms late at night and making off with any wallets and jewelry lying about. The riskier the plan, the better he liked it. Thanks to Brendan's discretion, Billy never got a chance to show just how truly imprudent he could be. And since neither ever did anything without the other, Billy had been protected so far from his own more outrageous instincts.

"What happened to your face?" Brendan asked when Billy arrived with blood still streaming from one nostril.

"Got hit with a truck name of Mickey McCormick. That's okay, though. Mick is singing in a higher key than he used to."

Brendan shook his head as if bemused by the quirks of an irrepressible younger brother. But there was nothing familial about the two young men. Billy was blond and pink-skin, Brendan dark-hair and ruddy—not homely but with none of Billy's angelic looks.

"Don't get blood on the carpet," Brendan said, returning his attention to a basketball game on the TV.

Billy lay down on the cot that doubled as Brendan's sofa and tilted his head back to stop the flow of blood. He spent as much waking time in this room as he did in his mother's apartment, and it felt even more like home. But he couldn't live without a woman to look after him, even if it was one with a heart condition. Brendan, by contrast, had been on his own since he was sixteen. His mother didn't even live in the neighborhood. He collected rents for her and was supposed to look after the building, though the tenants had long since given up expecting any janitorial services beyond his pushing the garbage cans out to the curb twice a week. But nobody was late with the rent more than once.

"Who's winning?"

"Boston. The Knicks can't do nothing right."

"Figures."

Brendan took another swig of beer, having apparently forgotten Billy's adventure in the funeral parlor. But then he asked, "Cath-a-leen there?"

"Yeah, why?"

"Just wondering."

"Right, like you wouldn't like to get inside her pants."

"Who said anything about getting inside her pants?"

"I know how your dirty little mind works, McCauley. Forget it. Cath-a-leen's a fucking lady. She don't go out with scumbags like us."

"Speak for yourself, kid."

"I'm speaking for both of us."

"Is that right?"

In one motion Brendan was out of the broken armchair he had been straddling and was on top of Billy.

"Jesus Christ, can't you see my fucking nose is bleeding?"

"What makes your sister so special, Billy? Didn't I tell you she already put out for me?"

"You're full of shit."

"Twice."

"In your fucking dreams."

"One of these days I'm gonna get the whole thing."

"You wish. How about getting off my chest before I fucking bleed to death?"

Brendan stared down at the pink cheeks streaked with bright blood, and grinned.

"Better stuff some toilet paper up there before you bleed all over my expensive furniture."

Brendan's lust for Billy's sister was a running joke between them and a sure-fire way of riling Billy. He was never quite sure how serious Brendan was about his designs on Cathleen. Nor did he know why he should care. He never kept tabs on the men Cathleen went out with from her office, except to assure her they were all pansies. But that was just to get her goat. In reality, he wanted her to find a nice rich guy and settle down, preferably taking their mother with her, even though that would leave him on his own without any legal means of support.

Apart from Cathleen, Brendan showed little interest in the opposite sex. Skin flicks from the video store seemed to satisfy all his sexual needs—nasty stuff too rough for Billy's tastes. Occasionally he dropped by Rosemary Grady's or one of the other sure things in the neighborhood, but as far as girlfriends were concerned Billy had never seen or heard of any. Ever since he was a kid, Brendan had been totally independent. Self-sufficient. Like Billy himself would like to be.

"Jimmy Duggan says there's some good shit on 17th Street. From Afghanistan," Brendan said at the next commercial break.

"Thanks, I'll pass."

"Scared?"

"Let's just say I'm getting prudent in my old age."

Brendan laughed at the idea of Billy Conover becoming prudent about anything, least of all drugs. Billy had OD'd twice on smack, his heart stopping the second time for several minutes in the ER. Afterward, he told Brendan he had seen his father and Jesus beckoning to him in white robes. But when he awoke to find a plastic tube stuck up his penis, another in his arm and a powerful pain in his chest where two interns had been pumping his chest, he only grinned up at the white coats and quipped, "What's up, Docs?"

Even so, the OD took some of the wind out of his sails—not because he had a cardiac arrest but because of that vision of his father waiting for him on the other side. As a Catholic he feared death because death could mean hell—was more *likely* to mean hell if you had done some of the things he had done. If he really was dead for the few minutes it took the doctors to get his heart going again, then what Jesus and his father were calling him to was the Day of Judgment. And he had no illusions that in the hereafter he could get away with the kind of mischief he had been able to persuade the cops and judges to overlook in this life strictly on the strength of his lily-white good looks and Irish moniker.

His mother was already asleep by the time he returned home, thanks to medication she received regularly from Dr. Mendelbaum, the family physician since before her husband died. She visited his office every month. He checked her blood pressure, listened to her heart and wrote a prescription for more angina pills and tranquilizers. She paid him out of the money Cathleen gave her. Most of her welfare check went toward paying the rent—rather, one third of the rent, which was all the Department of Social Services allowed her—with a small amount left over for food and other expenses. She also got food stamps but sold them to a neighbor because she was ashamed to use them on 9th Avenue where everyone knew her.

Billy gently closed the thin entrance door behind him. There was no light showing—it was past midnight—so he figured he had slipped in undetected. He tiptoed into the living room and lay down on the old sofa. But he had no sooner gotten comfortable than the bare overhead bulb suddenly came on and his sister appeared under its blinding light like an avenging angel from the Old Testament. Her hands were placed squarely on the hips of her pale blue nightgown, making her look a little flatfooted for an emissary of the Almighty. She had no makeup on, and as his eyes grew accustomed to the brilliance surrounding her, he was amazed to find her skin was no longer the immaculate perfection he remembered it to be.

"You realize you humiliated me in Roche's tonight?" she said as he was still marveling that his beautiful big sister was beginning to age. "Don't you have any shame? Don't you care about my feelings at all?"

"Piss off, Sis," he replied, turning away from the light and the human decay it had revealed. "He got what was coming to him."

"What about me? Did I get what was coming to me too? How do you think I felt, seeing you walk in there unshaven, not even dressed properly. Drunk."

"I wasn't drunk, just a little high."

"Do you think I want to be known as your sister? Do you realize I had to apologize for what you did? How do you think I felt?"

"You don't have to apologize for nobody," he said, his face to the wall, hugging the greasy pillow which, along with an old navy blanket, were the only bedclothes he slept with.

"Look at you. You're twenty-three years old. You're not a kid anymore. But do you have any kind of a job? No. Do you care? No. You should be ashamed of yourself. Why, I couldn't even bring anyone into this house if I wanted to."

"Like one of those fairies you go out with?"

There was silence for a moment. He knew the look on her face had changed from outrage to hurt, an alteration he had been able to effect at will ever since they were kids. But there would be no wrestling match as there might have been five or ten years ago, just the bitter complaint of an unmarried woman with a sick mother and shiftless brother on her hands.

"You got a fucking nerve."

He turned to face her. Her complexion seemed ravaged by dark blotches, old acne scars, and a dried-out look he associated with much older women.

"You're a disgrace to this family," she said.

"Fuck you."

"Daddy would turn over in his grave if he could see what you've become."

"Leave Daddy out of it."

"Do you care what he would think? Do you really? If you do, why don't you go back to school and make something of yourself instead of hanging out with criminals and junkies? Do you think you're special just because you're a little smarter than most of the retards you associate with? Well, I'll tell you something, Billy Boy, you're right down there on the same level with Jinny McCormick and your pal Brendan. You're a bum is what you are. A bum, plain and simple."

"How would you like a fucking smack in the mouth?" he said, raising himself on one elbow.

"Why don't you try?"

"What's going on in here? Why are you two fighting?"

Their mother stood in the narrow doorway, supporting herself against the skewed frame, dressed in a faded housecoat. "Do you know what time it is, for the love of God?"

"Your charming son just got in. You can thank him for waking you."

"Bullshit. I was tryna get some sleep when she comes in here and starts calling me names."

"I didn't call you names. I just told you what you are."

"Please," their mother said, clutching the front of her housecoat, "don't fight. You're brother and sister."

"Don't you even care about your own mother?" Cathleen said. "Do you realize she has a heart condition because of you?"

"Cath-a-leen, my heart's been bothering me for years."

"Ever since your darling Billy started getting thrown out of every school he set foot in."

"Piss off. If you want to be a nun, why don't you join a convent?"

"If I did, who would look after you, never mind who would take care of Mom?" Cathleen said, standing over him the way the nuns used to do. They carried yardsticks in those days to whack you over the hands or clout you across the back of the head when you least expected it. But first they stood over you just as Cathleen was doing now, glaring down and telling you how, by talking in class or punching your neighbor, you were slapping Jesus in the face as he hung dying on the cross for your sins. Then they whacked you, to give you a small taste of what a crucifixion was like, a mere suggestion of the suffering you were causing the Lord God Almighty. It hurt like hell, but Billy had always refused to show pain. He even defied the nuns by sticking out his tongue or, when he was older, by telling them to go to hell. Surprisingly, the more he talked back, the less they hit him. But his impudence meant his mother was sure to be called in, and after one too many incidents she was told she had better find another school for him.

"I can't even think about getting married. You're still too much of a baby to look after Mom."

"That's as good an excuse as any," he said, turning back toward the wall. "I feel sorry for the poor bastard has to put up with you for a wife. I'd rather be boiled in oil."

"Children, please," their mother said. "You're all you have, just the two of you. You mustn't...fight...."

She clutched her chest more tightly and grimaced. Cathleen rushed to support her.

"Billy!"

He jumped off the sofa and ran to get his mother's medication. Then he and his sister helped her back down the long corridor and laid her gently on her old cot just as if there had never been a cross word between them. They had become used to her attacks—or at least understood what was happening and knew what to do for her. But there was always the danger this was the one that would kill her and, as semi-orphans already, her chest pains always sobered them out of their selfish quarrels.

When she was breathing easily again they kissed her and vowed they wouldn't fight anymore. Then they returned to their respective bedrooms. But no sooner was Billy resettled on the sofa than he heard the shuffle of slippers across the room's worn carpet.

"You see what you've done!" his sister hissed.

"Piss off, Cath-a-leen."

"Someday you'll be the death of her."

"I said, piss off!"

"And I hope you burn in hell for it!" she said, barely dodging the dirty pillow he let fly at her.

He tried to sleep but couldn't. He could have stayed at Brendan's but didn't want to watch his friend cook up his daily dose of heroin, a ritual as predictable as halftime for the basketball game he was watching. But he felt equally uncomfortable in this house where he had been raised. This was the room his parents had used as a bedroom when his father was alive. Even then it had to double as a living room— they slept on a high-rise—while he himself enjoyed full occupancy of the small bedroom where his sister now slept. In those days, Cathleen spent her nights in the doorless dining room where their mother now had her cot. Back then the new red sofa was only a place for him to doze off when he was allowed to stay up late to watch a Christmas special on the family's small black-and-white.

After his father died he gladly gave up his bedroom to Cathleen, even though it meant abandoning his sports posters and a view of the busty Puerto Rican across the airshaft. Assuming a place on the sofa meant he was taking on the role of man of the house. He loved the old slipcovers, which still smelled of the uncles and aunts who used to visit them. He liked the dirty, once-cream-colored walls and dark worn rug. He was even attached to the faded portrait of Jesus hanging between two drafty windows that looked out onto 16th Street. When he was younger, he offered prayers to it, asking the Savior's and his dead father's help to be a better boy.

But tonight he felt like a stranger in this room. There would be no sleep for him after what his sister had said. He would lie here until the sky grew pink over the parking lot across the street. Then there would be more recriminations before Cathleen left for work, along with suggestions from his mother that he call up an uncle to ask if he could use an extra hand around the shop. She would even offer to make him breakfast and, louse that he was, he would let her, when it should have been he cooking for her. No, he decided, better to go back to Brendan's—or anyplace other than here.

Except for Scully's the streets were deserted. The bar drew customers not only from surrounding neighborhoods, it hosted uniformed police and firefighters by the hundreds whenever a fallen comrade was waked in one of the local funeral parlors. On those occasions dozens of police cars, some with license plates from New Jersey and Connecticut, double-parked along 9th Avenue, half the cops packed into the bare-bones tavern, the rest spilled out onto the sidewalks, each with a quart container of beer in his fist. Apart from a few bottles of hard liquor for the shot-and-beer crowd, beer was the only drink you could purchase in Scully's. Asking for a mixed drink there was like asking for caviar at a hotdog stand.

Billy headed down the block in a darkening mood that only a handful of amphetamines could lighten. He didn't need his sister's harping to know he should be holding down a job. But where was he supposed to find one? It was humiliating to ask relatives for work, especially when they already treated you like some kind of bug and didn't even speak to you except as a favor to your mother. Besides, why should he spend his days screwing desks together, when he was smarter than ten factory workers put together? It was easier for a girl. All she had to do was learn how to type and any business in the city was looking to hire her. But who wanted a high school dropout like himself for anything but grunt work? He would rather join the Army if it came to that than kiss somebody's ass for minimum wage.

"Billy Boy!" someone called from a midnight-blue Trans Am. The windows were heavily tinted, but the driver's was rolled down halfway to reveal Tommy McCready, a classmate from Billy's Bishop Dodge days. Tommy's father owned two junkyards, so there was never any question of his own son going jobless. The elder McCready had also had the foresight not to die prematurely. "What you up to, Billy?"

"Same ol' same ol', Tommy Boy. A little of this, a little of that," he said, stepping closer to the car.

"How's your gorgeous sister? Still busting chops?"

24

"She gets her licks in. But I keep her in line."

Like Brendan, Tommy also had the hots for Cathleen although she was a year older than them.

"Where you headed, Billy? Wanna take a ride?"

He glanced at the backseat windows, but the tinted glass didn't give a clue to who might be behind it. Even so, he said, "Why not?"

The car's interior was maroon velour, the roof off-white. The air was thick with pot smoke.

"This here's my boy Joey"—Tommy pointed over his shoulder at the muscular young men seated next to Billy—"and Frankie."

"Pleased to meet ya," Joey replied, offering a thick hand. Frankie raised a clenched fist.

"Interest you in a beer?"

"Sure, why not?" Billy said as Frankie dug between his legs and came up with something imported—they were all the same to Billy—then handed him the stub of a marijuana joint.

"How about dessert? Joey, show my friend Billy what's on the menu."

After some hesitation, Joey produced a handful of variously colored pills and capsules.

"What have we here?" Billy sorted them out carefully on the young man's palm. "Do I get to pick one from column A and one from column B?"

"Take whatever you want," Tommy said.

Billy selected a familiar-looking red-and-yellow tablet and a brown one he did not recognize. He downed them with a swig of beer.

"This here's Bruno," Tommy said rather as an afterthought, indicating the young man riding shotgun. Bruno didn't even bother to glance at the new passenger.

They drove along the southern perimeter of Prospect Park passed the small Quaker Cemetery whose high fence kids still climbed just as Billy himself used to do, surprised sometimes by groups of Haitians or Dominicans on the other side offering blood sacrifice. In the morning, park rangers found both used condoms and decapitated chickens, along with the occasional goat's carcass.

When they turned onto Ocean Parkway, Billy asked what their destination was.

Frankie said, "Nigger hunting," and raised a Louisville slugger

25

off the floor.

"Any niggers in particular?"

Frankie nodded toward the front seat. Bruno turned his head half-way and said, "The nigger that give me this."

A nasty wound, half-bruise and half-scab, covered most of an otherwise unremarkable profile. The eye itself was barely open.

"You in, Bill?" Tommy asked.

The dope was beginning to take effect. Streetlight reflected in the parked cars along the parkway seemed like moonshine on a dark ocean. He and his companions were buccaneers sailing the blue main in search of plunder and a ripe wench or two. He wished Brendan were with him. But then he remembered that by now his friend was in the warm arms of his White Lady and wouldn't care if Billy existed or not.

"Sure, what the hell. A little nigger-hunting can be very bracing."

# CHAPTER THREE

There was hardly anyone out on the pedestrian mall beside the parkway. In good weather the benches were filled with Orthodox Jews from nearby high-rises, old-country types who worshipped the sun till their skin turned a wrinkled mulatto-brown. He and Brendan used to ride out to Coney Island on the parkway's bike path to pick up Puerto Rican girls. When the girls' boyfriends showed up, Billy scared them off with one of his crazy-acts, speaking in tongues and pounding his chest while frothing at the mouth—his specialty, and a marvel to those who knew he was only faking—shouting all the curses he knew in Spanish, Yiddish, Italian and Gaelic, and some he didn't know. If that didn't work, he took off his pants and began eating sand or swung like a demented ape from the beams beneath the boardwalk. When all else failed he yelled "Rape!" until the intruders left or the police showed up.

"Whereabouts these niggers live?" he asked as they turned onto one of the alphabet avenues—N or M, he couldn't tell.

"Flatbush," Tommy replied. "East Flatbush. Somewheres around there."

By now Billy was so high he didn't care where he was headed. Any place was better than listening to his sister's diatribes. With luck, he would only return home after she had left for work and not have to confront her again until the next evening.

When they turned onto Flatbush Avenue the scarface in the front seat murmured, "Somewheres along here."

A few blocks along they spotted four young blacks congregated near an intersection. They looked young to Billy, younger than any-body in the car. Old enough, though, to have weapons, guns even. In a fair fight they would be no match for baseball bats and Irish savagery. But who had a fair fight anymore?

"That's them," Scarface said, leaning forward eagerly. "Anyways, close enough."

Billy felt some of the same giddiness he felt when he was about to step through somebody's bedroom window—a mix of terror and in-tense, an almost orgasmic excitement. A voice in his head whispered he didn't have any quarrel with these black kids. It was the same voice that also warned him he had no business taking other people's prop-erty or, for that matter, yanking his wiener after the lights were out. But over the years the voice had become merely a part of the experi-ence, just as a certain kind of music went with horror movies he en-joyed. The voice didn't stand a chance against the rush of adrenaline he felt.

"I got the one in leather," he heard Frankie murmur as if he were offering words of love in his best girl's ear.

"You want a bat or chains?" he asked Billy.

"A bat, I guess. Is it a righty or lefty?"

Frankie handed him a thick Louisville Slugger without taking his eyes off the dark prey on the sidewalk. By now, the black kids had caught on that something was up. But the code required that they not just cut and run unless the car belonged to the police. They were, after all, black kids in a black neighborhood, even though it was one in the morning and the streets were deserted.

Tommy double-parked the Trans Am as if he were just stopping to pick up a pack of cigarettes. Then he got out of the car, keeping some-thing—it looked like a blackjack from where Billy was sitting—con-cealed behind his back. The black kids watched carefully but still didn't move.

Bruno opened the door on his own side of the car. He showed no weapon but, once outside the car, his hand dropped into the pocket of his leather jacket.

"Watch our backs," Billy heard someone say as Tommy and Bruno walked toward the four kids on the corner. When they were halfway there Frankie said, "You guys follow me, but one at a time," and stepped out of the car, keeping the baseball bat concealed behind the door.

By now the black kids were shifting about nervously, their eyes fixed on the two whites approaching them. If they ran now and their visitors turned out to be cops, they could be shot down and a story made up later that they had fled resisting arrest. But if they didn't make up their minds soon they might suffer an equally bleak fate.

"What are you waiting for, you dumb yams?" Billy whispered, his heart pounding.

Tommy had come within a few feet of the intersection. Bruno was half a step behind. Billy remained by the car, his own bat concealed behind the open car door just as Frankie was doing. Tommy said something to one of the black kids but was too far away for Billy to make it out. One of the kids, the oldest-looking, took a step forward as if to reply. Bruno advanced as well. The young black seemed to be trying to engage Tommy in a discussion. He was so intent on making his point that he was ignoring Bruno. By the time his friends alerted him to the danger, he was facing a large automatic pistol aimed squarely at his forehead.

For a moment, he stared back at the weapon defiantly. Then he started taking small backsteps as if confronting a poisonous snake that could be avoided by not making any sudden move. But Bruno matched each backstep with a step forward. The other blacks broke and ran.

Realizing he was out of room, the young man began protesting, addressing all his words now to Bruno who still had the automatic aimed at his brow.

Tommy stepped forward and swung wildly with his blackjack. The black kid staggered backward but did not fall. Tommy was advancing for a second try when a shot rang out so loud that Billy thought somebody must have set off a cherry bomb. The young man tumbled backward and fell into a heap against a gated storefront, his forehead oozing blood.

Bruno remained standing over him as if contemplating a second shot. Tommy grabbed his arm and yelled, "You stupid fuck! You know what you just done?" But Bruno looked as if he could stand there for the rest of his life relishing his handiwork. Tommy had to forcibly turn him back toward the car, open the door and push him inside. Everyone else was already waiting inside. Tommy paused only long enough to take a quick look around, then drove off at high speed.

They headed north on Flatbush, running every red light. Billy knew the only danger lay in being spotted by a police car, but they made it to Prospect Park safely.

Bruno was sitting expressionless in the front seat. Billy himself had watched the killing with no more sense of reality than if he had been looking at TV or a movie. Even after everyone had piled into the car and he glanced back for a last look at the bundle of limp flesh that had been a human being, he was more impressed by the rapidity with which a living creature could be reduced to nothingness than by the consequences which might lie ahead for himself. Even now, he still felt nothing for the dead youth. He wondered as the car sped past the bare trees in the park if he would feel any different if the victim had been white.

"I'll hop out any place along here."

Tommy darted an angry glance in the rearview mirror.

"What I mean is," Billy amended, "I think we should split up."

Tommy abruptly hit the brake.

"A couple youse get out with Billy. Bruno, give Billy the gun."

"What're you crazy? I paid four bills for this piece."

"Give him the fucking gun!"

Bruno passed the gun to Billy.

"I really need this," Billy said.

"Bury it. If we get picked up, we didn't even see you tonight."

Billy put the gun in his jacket and was out of the car before Tommy came to a full stop. At Tommy's urging the two other occupants of the back seat followed. They looked lost, though Billy knew exactly where he was—north of the carousel, not far from the zoo. He pointed west. "Go that way." They hesitated. He put his hand into his jacket pocket. "Go, or I blow your fucking balls off."

He headed into the woods next to the road. It was all uphill and darker than he would have believed possible. He slipped several times in the damp leaves. At the top, a fallen tree blocked the path. He started around it but, feeling the heft of the gun against his side, decided this was as good a spot as any to stash it.

He rubbed the barrel and grip against the leg of his pants to get rid of fingerprints, then looked for a burial place. The ground was cold and hard. All he had to dig with were sticks and his bare hands. He wanted to bury the gun deep, a foot or more, but had to be satisfied with less than half that depth. He could always come back later and do the job properly.

He spread dead leaves on the spot, then climbed over the fallen tree and started down the other side of the hill. The ground in the wide hollow below was covered by a deep blanket of mist. He hesitated, having seen the same phenomenon several years ago when he took Suzy Meegan here to unburden her of her virginity. One moment he was on top of her, too whacked out on Tuinols and cheap booze to care where or who he was with, and the next a white shroud was closing around him. He got so scared he climbed off her and began yanking up his pants as if his mother had just busted them.

"What's the matter, Billy? It was getting good."

To him it had seemed the hand of God was calling him to account for his sins with Suzy and Rosie and all the other innocents he had deflowered.

"Come back, Billy. Do it some more."

"I, uh, just remembered something," he said, his young limbs shivering. He ran all the way to Prospect Park West, the white fog clutching at his legs like damned souls trying to drag him down to hell. As he ran he recited the Act of Contrition.

Seen from up high tonight, the rolling mist looked eerily beautiful. But he seemed to see its beauty without feeling it. At first he didn't understand why, but then recalled that a young man lay slaughtered on a street corner in Flatbush. He told himself the victim was only a nigger and it was not as if Brendan or Tommy had died. But the feeling of no-feeling persisted. Behind it lay a kind of terror—not the fear he felt yesterday when he was confronted by the three Latinos in Manny's building; that kind of fear inspired action and ultimately rewarded him with the thrill of having outwitted fate. What he felt tonight was cold and strangely numbing.

He started down into the thick ground fog which seemed to receive him like a fellow specter, reaching almost to his waist. He no longer believed in hell, but he avoided looking directly into the mist lest he see the corpse of that black kid, its dead eyes following him as if he himself had pulled the trigger.

Above, the sky was clear but moonless, the earth and heavens having changed places, with clouds hugging the ground and the air above dry and solid. He could make out very little ahead except a few tall trees on a nearby hill and a white building that looked like the

Greek temples in his old history books. He decided to climb the hill and exit the park at 9th Street rather than take the more direct route out.

At the top of the hill he spotted a mound of trash piled against a thick tree trunk as if someone had overturned a garbage can. Up close, he saw the trash was actually a shopping cart full of plastic bags containing empty cans and bottles. Next to it a pile of old coats roughly corresponded to a human shape.

It struck him that he might be better off himself spending the rest of the night here in the park. If he tried to make it back to Brendan's he might run into a patrol car. The police were probably looking for any white male of a certain age. He knew several cops in the local precinct on a first-name basis, but they would question him just the same. He need only stay in the park until the sun came up and commuters started filling the streets. No one would notice one extra pedestrian at that hour.

He squatted against a tree a few yards from the sleeping vagrant, hoping to doze off just long enough to see the sun rising. But he was cold and the ground was damp and the buzz inside his head kept him thinking about things he would sooner forget.

Meanwhile, the homeless person slept peacefully under several layers of coats. Would he, or she, mind if a stranger borrowed a coat for a couple hours? And if he or she did, what of it?

He had seen a lot of homeless in the neighborhood recently. Most were black women who spent their nights in the armory on Eighth Avenue. But the winos who hung out on Bartel Pritchard Square and sometimes shared a pint of cheap booze with him preferred camping out in the park. He might even know the man or woman inside that thick cocoon.

He gently pried a thin blanket from the pile, then lifted a heavier coat along with it. They both smelled pretty bad, but he would only have to endure the odor for a couple hours.

Suddenly a head appeared like a turtle peeking out from its shell. Two eyes peered up fearfully at him.

"What you want? I got no money."

It was a woman's voice. Black.

"I just wanna borrow one of your coats."

"Get your own stuff. This here's mine."

But he could tell by the forced hostility in the voice that she was more afraid of him than she was of losing one of her coats.

"Okay," he said nevertheless. "So I'll freeze. Keep your precious rags."

He dropped the coat and blanket back on the pile and returned to his spot beneath the other tree. If she had been a man, he would have just taken what he needed. But, homeless or not, he didn't dare remove the property of a woman without permission.

He started to shiver. The night had been a disaster from start to finish. First that business with Mick McCormick in Roche's. Then the fight with his sister. Then the murder, which still seemed more dream than reality. But it was because of that very real dead man that he was sitting here freezing instead of sleeping in a warm bed. Maybe Cathleen was right. Maybe he ought to try to make something of his life. He knew guys who had gone back to school, even joined the police force and now were twirling nightsticks instead of mooching off their mothers and living for their next high.

But then he thought what Brendan would say: Why kiss ass and ride crowded subway trains when everything you needed was right there for the taking? Did he really want to substitute coffee breaks and tuna sandwiches for the thrills of burglary and drugs? Besides, telling Brendan he wanted out, that their life together—practically all the life either of them had—was over, was something he couldn't face. For better or worse he would have to go on as before, even if it meant occasionally freezing or putting up with his sister's nagging. To the world he was Crazy Billy, but he was also Crazy Billy to himself now. That he couldn't alter, no matter how many jackets and ties he put on.

"You still there?" he heard the vagrant say. "You want the coat, take it. Just remember to put it back."

"Thanks. I will."

"No problem."

He wrapped a coat around himself and hunkered down again. It had been a good thick coat and still gave good warmth.

"You on the streets long?" she asked.

"Me? Naw," he said, feeling better now. He was even able to believe, whatever trouble the day ahead held for him, he would be able to talk his way out of it. "How about yourself?"

"Two months. Plus one week."

"You picked the wrong time of year."

There was silence at first. Then she said, "I didn't choose to be homeless. I lost my apartment. Then I lost my job. Bosses ain't too crazy about your coming to work without a bath."

"Sorry."

Again there was silence. But then, in a friendlier tone, "You want another coat?"

"No, I'm fine. Thanks."

"You want another, take it."

"Okay."

"Good night."

# CHAPTER FOUR

He was used to waking up in strange bedrooms—not to mention strange living rooms, bathrooms and kitchens. But not since his brief career as a Boy Scout had he awakened under a tree.

The smell of the coat, a distillation of old sweat, mildew and something more fetid that every homeless person seemed to carry around like a stamp of their disreputable state, brought him back to the present.

He raised his eyes toward Monument Hill, where he had buried the murder weapon. A flock of white birds were foraging on its sleigh-worn face. He had scraped some of those brown trails himself, barely avoiding a broken limb any number of times, thanks to his bent for splitting the narrow passage between two treacherous trees known as the Needle that most other kids sensibly avoided.

It was hard to believe that a gun, one of its chambers recently spent on the destruction of a human life, now lay buried there by his own hands. It was even harder to believe he himself had played a part in the killing. He had been involved in plenty of criminal activity but, till now, none of it ever included murder.

He tested his limbs and found them stiff after just a few hours on the cold ground. The day seemed well under way, eight or nine o'clock, he guessed. It should be safe now to walk the streets. He could head home, change clothes, maybe take a shower and then lay low to see what developed.

He carefully returned the coat to the pile of old clothes. A hank of matted hair lay among the damp leaves like a discarded pennant. The pile suddenly began to move. A forehead and two dark eyes appeared.

"Who are you?"

"The guy you gave the coat to. I was just putting it back. Thanks very much."

"What do you want?"

"I don't want nothing," he said. "Don't you remember? You let me borrow the coat to keep warm."

"You better get out of here before I yell."

"Don't do that," he said, back-stepping. "I'm already leaving. See? I'm going."

He didn't look back until he had crossed the path leading up to the Greek-style Tennis House.

She was still watching him.


Meanwhile, Brendan McCauley was sitting in the Conover kitchen, nursing a cup of tea.

"I guess he must have slept over one of his friend's houses," he said to Billy's mother, trying to sound unconcerned. He had already heard about the shooting from a friend of Tommy McCready. There had also been something on the morning news. The reporter said a car filled with white kids had attacked a black gang over a bad dope deal. Tommy's friend said Billy was in that car—an unlikely scenario, Brendan thought, since Billy avoided violence the way he avoided honest labor. Even so, he thought he might just pay a visit to the Conover household, where he had at least one fact confirmed: Billy had left the house late in the evening and had not returned.

"I'm sure he'll turn up anytime now, Mrs. C."

"I expect you're right, Brendan. Though I don't mind telling you, I still worry about him even though he's a grown man. I imagine your own mother probably worries as well. I mean when you're late or she doesn't hear from you."

"She sure does, Mrs. C.," Brendan said, though in fact his mother didn't know if he was dead or alive from one week to the next and probably didn't care as long as she got her rent receipts.

"I'd rest a whole lot easier if he would just get a job like the other boys. You're his best friend, Brendan. Do you suppose you could have some influence on him? He's always looked up to you, you know, ever since you were little."

"Is that right, Mrs. C.?"

"He should be working. Like you do, Brendan."

"Well, Mrs. C., I don't really do all that much, you know."

"You support yourself, don't you? You can't do that without money. And you earn it yourself. You don't depend on your mother like he does. I don't know what would become of that boy if anything happened to me. I couldn't depend on Cath-a-leen to look out for him. I know she wouldn't let him starve. But she has a life of her own. She can't be expected to look after him for the rest of her life."

"You got a point there, Mrs. Conover," Brendan said, recalling the last time he had seen Cathleen Conover, at a wedding reception. She was dressed in a blue mini-length cocktail dress with what, for that neighborhood, was a pretty daring neckline. He still had wet dreams about that dress.

"Talk to him, Brendan," Mrs. Conover said, leaning across the old iron-top table and smiling a smile which in her youth had charmed many a young man into doing her bidding.

"I will, Mrs. C. But don't expect no miracles. By any chance, did Billy say where he was heading last night?"

"Not as far as I know. I was in bed myself. I wasn't feeling well. My angina, you know. They had a little squabble, his sister and him. I went to bed then. I thought everybody else did too. But then I wake up this morning and he's gone." She sat back with a sigh. "I suppose I could call his sister at her job. But I try not to bother her."

"Sure, I understand. I was just thinking, maybe it would help me locate him for you if I knew where he was headed."

Mrs. Conover smiled maternally.

"You're such a nice young man. Always trying to be of help. You were always that way, Brendan. Your mother must be proud of you."

"I'm just doing what any friend would do, Mrs. C."

"I know you are. And don't think I don't appreciate it," she said, refilling his cup with hot water and dropping the same used teabag back in it. "I'll bet you'd like a couple cookies to go with your tea, wouldn't you?"

"Don't go to no bother on my account."

Brendan visited Rosemary Grady next, just a few doors down from Scully's where she occasionally popped in for a quart container when the kids were napping. There were, in fact, two cylinders of the type Scully's provided for its endless supply of Budweiser standing on the floor beside her kitchen table, one of which was being used to store her three-year-old's toy cars.

"What brings you around, Brendan? Don't tell me it's my great conversation."

It was past eleven, but she had not yet combed her dirty brown hair. He could smell it as he watched her burn some fried eggs on a stovetop that contained traces of every meal she had cooked for the past two years. She had on a faded pink bathrobe that emphasized her wide hips and full breasts.

"Billy Conover didn't come home last night. I thought maybe he stayed here."

She glanced at him with a hung-over version of her come-hither smile. Part of Rosemary's reputation had to do with that smile. She got it from her mother who never so much as entertained an evil thought during the course of her fifty short years in this world. Rosemary's mother got it from her own mother, an immigrant from County Mayo and a faithful wife. Rosemary's Aunt Kate or, as she was known to the religious world, Sister Mary Katherine, had the same smile and no one ever expected to get a blow job because of it.

"So Billy goes missing one night, and right away you think he's with Rosemary? No such luck. The longest he ever stayed here was a half-hour. That was the time my old man turned up and Billy had to make a quick exit through the yard.

"So you ain't heard from him?"

"Not a word, Brendan. But you can tell him from me he's welcome to come around."

She flipped the eggs out of the pan and onto a paper plate which had also held last night's franks and beans. Then she called her three-year-old to the table. He brought the plastic beer container with him. His sister was asleep in the dark middle room of the apartment. The three of them lived off Welfare, although Rosemary's landlady could have raised the rent at any time and put them out on the street—or more likely into a homeless shelter, since Rosemary had no one left who would take her in.

"Sure you wouldn't like a cup of coffee?"

"No, thanks. I got a message for Billy. Maybe if you hear from him you'll tell him I need to see him right away."

"Sure," she said, then shouted, "Billy!" as if her sometimes lover were in the next room.

Brendan waited, his hand on the doorknob, to see if the man himself would materialize.

"Billy Boy, get your ass over here."

The child under the table jumped to his feet, two dented toy cars in his hands. He had big blue eyes. Rosemary's were small and dark. His hair was the color of young corn. His mother's was mousy brown. Rosemary's ex-husband was a local boy who was doing seven-to-fifteen for Armed Robbery plus a concurrent for Possession with Intent. He was a short, ugly guy who no more resembled this child than Brendan himself did.

"Eat!"

"See you around, Rosy."

He headed back to Scully's. The bar was a clearinghouse for information—whose brother got arrested for what, whose sister got knocked up by who. The only thing you couldn't do there was cop dope. The management would beat your head in and then call the cops besides if it found you even dealing a loose joint on the premises.

At this time of day the bar was given over to the boilermaker crowd, old guys with red, deeply pocked faces who looked like they wouldn't last another week but showed up every day for their shots and beers as religiously as their wives did for mass. This wasn't a likely time to run into somebody who might know where Billy Conover was. But you never knew who might turn up at Scully's on any given day. The sun was breaking through the late-morning overcast. Streams of yellow light bathed the brick facades of the buildings on 9th Avenue. As a kid, Brendan used to play with poster paints. He also liked to draw in his spare time, which was most of his time after he dropped out of Bishop Dodge. He rarely did so anymore, unless it was to do an obscene cartoon. But he still noticed a pretty patch of sky and admired the first flowering of the trees in Prospect Park. This morning, though, he was too preoccupied to give the pretty play of color more than a passing glance.

The bar smelled the same day and night, as if they hosed down the floor and walls with beer. There were only three customers there this morning. Two were old duffers, with an all-too-familiar younger face halfway down the long mahogany. Brendan was already through the door and would only arouse suspicion if he walked out again.

"Charlie! How's it going?" he called, offering his hand eagerly, as if this old classmate did not pack a .38 Police Special under his jacket.

"Ain't it a little early in the day for you?" Charlie Madigan replied.

Brendan laughed as if the young cop had said something genuinely witty.

"I just come in to get some change for a call. Goddamn phone went dead."

"Maybe you forgot to pay the bill," Charlie said, sipping a beer and looking the way cops did when they wanted you to think they could read your mind.

"Nah. Them suckers been fooling around with the line. Same thing happened to the family below me. The phone company opens up that box on the corner and, boom, down go half a dozen other phones wasn't even broke."

Charlie laughed. Round-faced, not yet overweight but starting to put it on around the kidneys just like the other Madigans, he had the kind of clear blue Irish eyes that Brendan had always envied.

"What brings you in here yourself?"

Charlie shrugged, took another sip and said, "You never know. Sometimes you pick up a piece of useful information."

"You guys are always on the job. Don't you ever just take a day off?"

"Like I said, you never know."

He glanced at Brendan as if to say there was no use trying to put one over on a cop. It was a dangerous look because when police looked at you that way it was frequently followed by a cuff on the side of the head or something worse.

"What's Billy Conover up to these days?"

Brendan put his foot up on the brass rail. There were no stools in Scully's and never had been. He raised a finger to indicate the beer tap to the bartender.

"He got hooked up with some kind of training program."

"That right?"

"Something Cath-a-leen helped him find. Welding or something."

"Glad to hear it. He ain't no kid anymore. I guess you heard what happened in Roche's the other night."

Brendan tried to look as if he had to think hard to remember.

"That little scuffle with Jinny McCormick's brother?"

"Scuffle? He damn near broke Mickey's balls. The people I talked to said Billy was high."

"No way. Billy don't do nothing but smoke a joint now and then. He's clean."

"Sure he is. And if I believe that, you'll tell me a better one. Right, Buzzy?"

Brendan was more than willing to treat the subject as a joke. But the use of his old nickname brought to mind a cold afternoon in the yard of Holy Family several years earlier. Being a serious type even then, Charlie had taken some words about his mother very personally—Billy had either questioned her premarital virginity or personal hygiene, Brendan couldn't remember which—and was chasing Billy around the schoolyard. Billy kept up the tease until Charlie was reduced to breathless tears, his nose running down the front of his oversize parka. It was classic Billy. He never laid a hand on the kid and, thanks to his nimble feet, his victim never had a prayer of doing any harm to his tormentor. That was fifteen years ago, but Brendan knew the incident probably still rankled the young cop more than if Billy had beaten his brains out.

"Hey, I lead my life and Billy leads his. You know what I mean? I got a whole building to look out for."

"Keeps you busy, putting out the garbage and stuff?"

"It's the little things. A broken washer. A fucking pipe busts."

"Keeps you going day and night."

"And all I get for it is a free apartment and a few bucks for food. As soon as this here recession is over, I'm gonna get me a real job. My old lady can take her building and stuff it."

Brendan could feel the beer now, and with it the inspiration only alcohol or drugs could provide. He would be content to stand here all day and hold forth. But he knew he'd better leave before he said something he shouldn't, so he hastily downed the rest of his beer.

"You ain't happened to see Billy today, have you?" Charlie asked.

"Naw. Like I said, me and Billy, we been going our separate ways. That's how it is. But I gotta run," he said, slapping a dollar bill on the bar, having completely forgotten the phone call he had said he needed to make. "Tenant got a broken radiator."

# CHAPTER FIVE

Charlie watched Brendan walk out of the bar with a mixed feeling of nostalgia and bitterness. Billy and Brendan had been a plague on his life throughout his grammar school days. Not only were there those teasings in the schoolyard; there were any number of mean little tricks, like the time they put cat shit in his lunch pail or farted in the rectory and told the priest it was he who had done it. He used to lie awake late into the night imagining an elaborate vengeance he would take, especially on Brendan who seemed to derive a perverse pleasure from the pain his friend caused.

But it was hard to feel the same animosity toward Billy Conover. Something about the son-of-a-bitch remained persistently likeable, even when he was busting your chops or conning you out of your last quarter. The report of the killing in East Flatbush had included a description of a car driven by a white male. The same witness said a thin blond youth was also present. There were thousands of people in Brooklyn who fit that description. Billy was a good-for-nothing, never worked a day in his life, lived off his sister and his mother. But he was no killer.

One more dead shine meant nothing to Charlie. If blacks were out on Flatbush Avenue at one, two o'clock in the morning, they were looking for trouble. But his cop's instincts told him Billy Conover knew something. That was why, on his day off, he had decided to spend some time in Scully's. And sure enough, Brendan had turned up, looking for Billy.

Charlie headed down 16th Street and turned in at the second house on the right.

"Hello, stranger. What brings you to this neck of the woods?"

Rosemary had changed out of her long cotton nightgown and into tight jeans and a blue turtleneck that showed off her breasts.

"Just old times sake, Rosy. My day off."

She didn't turn away from the pail of dirty wash she was sorting to ask, "You ain't got something else on your mind? 'Cause I got to get this little monster to the doctor for a measles shot. Otherwise he don't get into pre-K, and that means he drives me crazy till the next semester."

"No problem," Charlie said.

He actually did have nothing but business on his mind when Rosemary showed him in. But he had to admit that her nicely-rounded, if a bit over-inflated rear end did put other ideas in his head. He had never been a regular visitor to Rosemary's, even back in the days before the arrival of her first kid put a damper on her generosities. But before his marriage to Cynthia Cavanaugh, former Queen of the May, he, like several other young men in the neighborhood, knew Rosy was a safe port when the only alternative was a sticky copy of *Playboy*.

"You working nights?" she asked, filling a pillowcase with small pants, shorts and underwear so badly soiled they temporarily drove any sexual thoughts from Charlie's mind.

"One week I work days, the next week nights. Keeps me on my toes."

"Jesus, I wouldn't want to be married to you," she said, causing him an unaccountable pang of remorse. He was, he thought, happily if routinely married, with a child on the way. "Must drive your wife crazy."

"She's used to it. It goes with the job," he said with pride.

"Even so. I can't get a decent night's sleep as it is. I can't imagine what it would be like if I had my whole day turned upside down as well."

Charlie had known Rosemary's husband—a tough, wild kid, dumb as whale turd. But Rosemary herself was no dope except when it came to keeping her legs closed. It had been just a matter of time before she or her old man skipped out of the marriage.

"I'd offer you a cup of coffee, only, like I said, I'm kind of in a hurry."

"I just stopped by to see if maybe you heard from Billy Conover," he said, staring down at the blond, blue-eyed boy she was dressing. The same thought went through his mind that had passed through Brendan's an hour earlier.

"What's the matter, he done something?"

"I just happen to be talking to Brendan in Scully's. He ain't seen Billy in a couple days, so I thought I'd ask around."

"Scully's? What the hell's Brendan doing in Scully's at this time of day?"

Charlie shrugged innocently.

"What were *you* doing in Scully's? Your old lady lets you go to bars in the daytime?"

"Hey, it's not like I'm putting away boilermakers like them old farts that hang out there. I had a beer, that's all."

Rosemary straightened up and swept her long brown hair back from her face, her breasts swinging freely beneath the turtleneck. A glisten of perspiration clung to her lips and cheeks. She was still one of the best-looking pieces of ass around, Charlie decided, and here she was saddled with two kids and no husband. For two cents, he would fuck her right now, wife or no wife, despite the stench of diaper shit and the roaches scampering across the oilcloth.

"Naw, I ain't seen Billy. I ain't seen nobody for a while, if you know what I mean. Two's enough." She nodded toward the bags of dirty wash. "You know what it's like tryna live on the bullshit check Welfare sends you?"

"Must be tough," Charlie said.

"If it wasn't for food stamps and the little bit my sister sends me, I'd be up shit's creek." She shook her head. "It takes a while, but I learned. No more babies. You know how old I'm gonna be before this one "—she jerked a finger toward the baby sleeping in a battered portable crib—" is ready to go out and get a job?"

"It's tough," Charlie said, his swollen penis lodged uncomfortably between his right pocket and scrotum. He reached casually under the table to free it.

"So," Rosemary said, giving him a grin which suggested she knew exactly what was happening inside his pants, "you can spread the word around, Charlie: Old Rosy's retired. At least from serious fucking. I ain't saying," she added confidentially, "I wouldn't do a blow job now and then. But it's strictly cash and carry. Now, if you don't mind, I gotta get this kid to the doctor."

Charlie pushed his chair back from the kitchen table. His ordinarily pale, almost translucent skin, looked like it had just spent a couple hours in subfreezing weather or had had his cheeks slapped by Sister Bernice. His erection was stiffer than ever, but he had no alternative, so he stood up and began zipping up his jacket, hoping his tight jeans would conceal his excitement.

"If you do see Billy, give him my regards," he said, trying to sound like the canny cop.

"Sure thing, Charlie." She gave him another grin, dropped her eyes to his crotch and winked. "And you give mine to Cynthia."

Billy stood at the window and watched Charlie walk back toward the corner of 9th Avenue.

"For a minute I thought you was gonna ream him out right on the kitchen table."

"Gimme a break."

"You gonna tell me you never sucked Charlie off?"

He was watching the street below and missed the pained response in Rosemary's eyes.

"Listen, Billy. I let you stay here and hide like some kid playing hooky, when I don't even know what it is you did."

"Who said I did anything?"

"I had a fucking cop sitting right here in my kitchen. If I wanted to I could have put your ass in jail."

"I told you, I didn't do nothing."

"Then, why'd you come here? And how come you looked like you was gonna shit in your pants when I said it was Charlie Madigan coming up the stairs?"

Satisfied that Charlie wasn't coming back, Billy turned away from the window only to find Rosemary stripped down to her bra and panties. She had closed the louver door that separated her bedroom from the dark middle room and kitchen where the boy had returned to his toy cars.

"What's this?"

She lowered the waistband of her baby-blue underwear and struck a pose like a gun moll in an old movie. "As long as you're here..."

"You said you was retired. Ain't that what you just told Charlie?"

he said, stepping closer and reverently drawing her panties down to her ankles before genuflecting in front of her. She put her hands on his shoulders and said, "Jesus, Billy, I love it when you do that. I love it better than anything."

"I shall go to the altar of God...." he said. The baby woke up, but Rosemary paid him no mind. "To God who giveth joy to my youth."

# CHAPTER SIX

There was no mention of the killing in the early editions of the *News* or *Post*. But by midday the story had the entire front pages. Not being an avid reader, Billy only learned how much publicity the murder was receiving when one of the regulars at the OTB asked, "You hear where they blew away that yam in Flatbush?"

Billy asked to see the story and found the details were wrong. The "trigger man" was described as over six-foot and blue-eyed. The same story said the driver was Hispanic and that some black youths had tried to intervene to save their friend. But the description of the car was close enough and whoever gave the information could at least count because they spotted five people inside it.

"I hear Tommy McCready was in on it," the old junkie confided sotto voce.

"Who?"

"McCready, from 22nd Street. He pals around with the guineas in Bensonhurst."

"I ain't seen Tommy lately, but he ain't the sort to go nigger-hunting."

"I hear it wasn't nigger-hunting. I hear they was out to make a big score and the yams stiffed them."

"That right? Well, you just can't trust nobody anymore. Hey, I'd like to stay and chew the fat, but I gotta run. Thanks for the ups. I'll remember you in my will."

Billy headed for Brendan's house. Be cool, he thought. Act like nothing's happened. He had spent the night with Rosemary. She would vouch for him, God bless her. His mother and sister would swear he had been at home before that. He would chill out at Brendan's, maybe grab a nap and save the ups for later. That way he wouldn't have to go out for the rest of the day.

"Where the fuck you been?" Brendan greeted him.

"Here and there. You got beer?"

"I been looking high and low for you. Charlie Dickface was asking about you. Where you been, Billy Boy?"

"First things first, Brendan. Open a cold one for your old pal. Confessions don't start for another ten minutes."

He flopped down on Brendan's sprung sofa.

"Get your own fucking beer. Did you know some assholes snuffed a nigger over in Flatbush last night?"

"I read something like that in the daily gazette."

"The word is, Tommy McCready had something to do with it. You wasn't along for the ride, by any chance?"

"Me? Engage in violence against a fellow human? Billy the Meek? Billy the lover of spics, yams and all the other lower forms of life? How about getting me that beer, shithead?"

"Jesus. You look like you slept in the park."

Billy regarded his clothes with concern.

"Smell like it too. Come on, man, what you been up to? Your mother said you left the house after midnight and you ain't been home since."

"Excuse me, please, but did someone appoint you my keeper?"

Brendan approached the sofa and took hold of his friend's shirtfront.

"I want the truth, Billy. If you was with McCready and those other assholes, you could blow us sky-high."

"I don't think Rosemary Grady would appreciate your referring to her as an asshole."

"You spent the night with Rosemary? Where'd the two of you sleep, the horse stables?"

"We did have a romp in the hay."

"I'm warning you, Billy. You tell the truth or you're out on your ass right now. Let your mother and Cath-a-leen front for you. I ain't getting mixed up in no murder."

"Relax, Brendan. I told you, there's nothing to worry about."

His shirt was beginning to pinch at the armpits.

"There better not be, Billy. So help me. If you *was* mixed up and it brings the cops sniffing around, you know what that means."

"I'm not that stupid. Now, how about that beer? And I'd appreciate a little peace and quiet. I had a very vigorous night, thanks to the lovely Rosemary."

Brendan brought the beer as well as one for himself but was too preoccupied to open it.

"How about turning on the TV?" Billy said.

"I thought you wanted sleep."

"That's why I want the TV on."

Brendan shook his head in disgust but switched on the old television set lodged between a pair of windows identical with the Conovers' facing 16th Street.

"What channel?"

"Don't matter," Billy said as the screen showed two lovers in a soap opera having an argument. "That's good."

Brendan shook his head again and sat down.

The lovers, both beautiful in an exaggerated saccharine way, seemed more concerned with their camera angles than with the credibility of their characters. But Billy's mind was on the events of the night before and his options for the days ahead.

He could kick himself for agreeing to take the gun. He could also kick himself for getting into Tommy McCready's car in the first place. If he hadn't had that argument with his sister, he would have spent the night on the sofa in his mother's apartment. He would have read about the killing the next day as an interested but innocent citizen instead of someone the cops might be looking for. He blamed Cathleen for his predicament. She never let up, bitching every chance she had about his not having a job. Didn't she realize there was a recession on? What was he supposed to do, collect cans and bottles from garbage pails like the neighborhood glue-head? He never asked her for money— well, almost never. And he hardly took any from his mother, no more than what he needed for carfare or a few ups in an emergency when he and Brendan had to lay low for a while.

"You heard I said Charlie Madigan was asking for you in Scully's?" Brendan said.

"How is old Charlie? Still pissing in his pants?" he said, thinking of the time he and Brendan had cornered Charlie on the school roof and threatened to throw him off.

"I wouldn't joke if I was you. He was talking like he had suspicions."

"Relax, Bren. I told you, I was with Rosemary."

"He had a look in his eye. Like he smelled a promotion, you know?"

"Charlie was a snot-nose jerk when he was ten, and he still is. If I say boo to him he'll shit in his pants."

"Not if he has his gun."

"I could still take him with one arm tied behind my back."

On the TV, a heavily made-up nurse was giving in to the persistent charms of a swarthy intern.

"Are you gonna drink that beer, by any chance?" Billy asked. "Cause if you ain't, I don't mind relieving you of it."

Brendan regarded the unopened can in his hand as if it were a pigeon that had lighted there without his noticing. He passed it to Billy.

"Thanks."

Billy reached into his shirt pocket, came up with two yellow pills and popped them in his mouth. But he knew two would do nothing more than relieve the depression he could feel coming on the way an arthritic can sense approaching weather.

"What time you got, Bren?"

"Half past eleven."

"If I fall asleep, make sure I'm up by five."

"You got a date or something?"

"Could be. Now be a good fellow and let me catch forty winks. The beauteous Rosemary can suck the energy right out of a man."

Billy awoke to the sound of footsteps in the stairwell outside Brendan's apartment. His first thought was that it was the police, but then he heard the giggles of teenage girls. He looked out the living room window at the sky above the one-family houses across the street. A weak sun was trying to break through the clouds. He could hear some kids playing football in the street below.

He got up, drained the remains of the beer he had started earlier and looked around for his jacket. Being seen in the neighborhood might be risky. On the other hand, not being seen at all could make it seem he was trying to hide. Besides, he would go stir crazy if he spent any more time alone in Brendan's apartment. There had to be a place he could go till it got dark and he could slip back into the park to dig up the gun and hide it in a safer place.

When he was a kid and got into trouble he didn't dare go home because his mother would be waiting for him, having already gotten a telephone call from the principal or offended neighbor. Meek as she was about most of his peccadilloes, she would not abide his showing disrespect to clergy or to neighbors on the block.

That was when he used to flop at Brother Timothy's. Brother Tim was not like the other faculty at Dodge—uptight and always coming down on you for the least little thing. He seemed more like one of the students, although even in those days he must have been middle-aged. Billy still saw him taking his afternoon walk through the neighborhood, his head down, dressed in old clothes and rarely bothering to shave. People who didn't know better took him for a bum.

8th Avenue was residential and therefore less trafficked than busy 9th Avenue, but he kept his scarf up around his face. The intersection at 17th Street was a long-time junkie's haven. You could still cop a bag of heroin or crack there, but the precinct kept a much closer watch than they used to and the shooting galleries had all been turned into co-ops.

He nodded at a lookout loitering outside a corner bodega but continued on to the footbridge spanning the Prospect Expressway. The bridge used to be a favorite spot for him and Brendan to shake down fellow students, threatening to throw them onto the highway if they didn't pay up. Today he had the crossing to himself.

"What brings you to visit this old man?"

The once-robust Brother Timothy seemed permanently hunched over, as if time were slowly crushing him under its weight. His still bright blue eyes watered constantly. His thin hair was white, his cheeks blotchy red. He was wearing a pair of old jeans and a flannel shirt that might have been made for a man twice his size.

"Just old time's sake, Brother," Billy said, already having second thoughts about the visit. He wasn't even sure the man still had all his marbles.

But then the cleric regarded him with a knowing smile that recalled a younger, more vigorous man who could see through boys like

Billy better than they could each other.

"Well, maybe a little more than old times sake," Billy admitted. "Maybe I wanted to have, you know, a talk. Like we used to."

Brother Timothy sat back in the big swivel chair that held him like a frail child. He seemed in no hurry to find out what crisis had brought his former student to consult with him. He asked about Billy's mother.

"She still has trouble with the ticker. But half the time I think she makes it up just to get me to do what she wants."

"Do you—do what she wants?"

"Usually.... Well, most of the time.... Well...sometimes."

The two men, one nearing the end of life, the other closer to its beginning, regarded each other silently. Then a familiar grin lit up Brother Timothy's face. At first Billy resisted its subversive appeal, but soon gave in.

"I guess I still can't B-S you, Brother T."

"You probably can, but not about your mother."

Billy recalled the man who used to play basketball with the boys and break up fights, plunging right into the fracas like he wouldn't know a roman collar from a tiara. More than once he caught a punch intended for a student. Billy once hit him by accident himself and made his nose bleed. But Brother Timothy never seemed to hold such mishaps against anyone and showed as much good will toward the worst of his charges as he did toward the better behaved.

"Do you mind if I ask a personal question, Brother?"

"Why not?"

"I was wondering, did you ever wish you had, you know, gone on to become a priest?"

"No. Not once."

"But don't you ever miss, you know..."

"Playing God? That was exactly what I didn't want. I wasn't cut out for the priesthood, Billy. Too much responsibility. I'm happy being a brother. I have no regrets." He regarded his visitor with a tired smile, as if the question were one he was frequently asked and never seemed able to answer to anyone's satisfaction. "But that's not what brought you here—to find out why I'm happy sweeping up the gym instead of hearing confessions."

"Not exactly. I have this here...problem."

"What else is new."

"This time it's a real problem, Brother Tim. With a capital P."

The old man's eyes seemed to grow brighter. Suddenly he looked twenty years younger. "I'm all ears."

Billy began to describe in a roundabout way the difficulty he had gotten himself into. He gave no names, did not even give a clear indication of the kind of crime he had been party to. But it was the first time since he had stopped going to confession eight years earlier that he had admitted any wrongdoing to an adult.

Brother Timothy regarded him placidly and said, "Why not just go to the police and tell them what you know—or don't know, as the case may be?"

"I don't think that would be a wise move. My reputation at the precinct ain't exactly what you would call an Eagle Scout's."

"Were you in the Scouts, Billy? Somehow I don't see you as the type."

"I was asked to retire on account of something I left in the scoutmaster's backpack. You see, Brother, I ain't never done nothing exactly, well, bad, if you know what I mean. But I been involved in certain activities from time to time that ain't exactly kosher as far as the law is concerned. So the cops ain't exactly gonna consider me what you might call an unimpeachable character when it comes to something like this."

Brother Timothy sat back and joined his hands on his small paunch. "How exactly can I be of help?"

"Well, I'm not sure. I just didn't know where else to turn. This is kind of uncharted territory."

"I can tell you one thing, Bill. If you don't level and tell me exactly what kind of trouble you've gotten into, there's not much I can do to help."

"I was afraid you was gonna say that."

"Well, you didn't come here for absolution, did you?"

"No, I guess not."

All of a sudden Billy noticed an all-too-familiar aroma. It was the smell of schools, churches and weekend retreat houses he remembered from when he was still under the authority of the nuns and priests. Nothing had ever made him more homesick than the smell of a disinfected dormitory, all the boys lying on their hard cots after lights-out, the priest or brother in charge walking up and down the space at the foot of their beds, clicking rosary beads.

He had some of that same homesick feeling now. This man, after all, had no home of his own, not even the inhospitable but reliable four rooms on 16th Street. There was something not right about this kind of life, even made someone who lived it suspect. Besides, why should he spill his guts to this old man? There was no privilege of the confessional. Brother Timothy was just a janitor who swept up priests' dirt.

"On second thought, maybe I should think it over for a while."

Brother Timothy's brow furrowed, but he said, "You know where I am if you change your mind."

"I sure do. And thanks, Brother. You may not think so, but I do feel better."

"I'm glad for that."

"You take care of yourself," Billy said, getting up and offering his hand.

Brother Timothy rose with some difficulty and never did manage to stand quite straight up. He smiled, but the twenty years he had lost a few moments ago had returned with a vengeance.

# CHAPTER SEVEN

"You don't gotta go to no trouble on my account, Mrs. Conover."

"It's no trouble, Charlie. I was planning to make myself a cup anyway. To tell you the truth, I'm glad for the company. Now that Billy and Cath-a-leen are both grown, it gets a little lonely around here. I'm happy to have someone to talk to—especially a nice young man like yourself. I'm sure your own mother must miss you now that you're married. But of course you're just around the corner from her, aren't you."

"That's right, Mrs. C. And pretty soon she'll have a grandchild to occupy her."

"Isn't that grand," Mary Conover said with genuine pleasure, turning on the gas under the same kettle she had been using for the last twenty years. "Wouldn't I love to hear the patter of little feet myself. But it seems Cath-a-leen is in no hurry to get married, and Billy... Well, I don't think he even has a girlfriend."

"Give them time, Mrs. C. One of these days they'll be walking down the aisle, and then you'll have more grandchildren than you know what to do with."

Mrs. Conover laughed, a silly girlish laugh, as if her guest were talking about her own prospects for childbearing. She had always been a bit flaky, Charlie recalled, flirting with her son's friends in an offhand way that had struck him odd even when he was a kid—not that he was such a frequent visitor to this house. His own mother was a down-to-earth woman who spent her days cleaning and scrubbing and right now was doing a load of wash for her daughter-in-law. Somehow she also managed to keep herself as tidy as her kitchen, while

Billy's mother looked like she was wearing the same ratty housecoat she had on ten years ago.

"I'm sorry Billy isn't here. I know that's who you really came to see, not this wrinkled old lady. I expect he'll be home for dinner. I can't always keep up with his goings and comings," she said as if talking to herself. But then remembering her visitor was a police officer, she added, "He goes job-hunting a lot. All over Brooklyn. Sometimes even into Manhattan."

She hadn't been to Manhattan herself since her sister Connie died and was waked in Cooke's on the Upper West Side. Connie had married an Italian butcher and lived like a queen. Mary Conover never cared for him.

"He was out of here first thing this morning. Early," she said, taking down a box of stale crumb cake from the top of the refrigerator. She placed it on the table between Charlie's teacup and her own. "Oh, he would do very well if only he could get a break."

Charlie scraped some sugar from the hardened remains in the cracked bowl and stirred it into his tea.

"He gets up early? That's a sure sign he has the right attitude, Mrs. C."

"At the crack of dawn. In fact, he was gone even before I was up myself this morning, and I'm an early riser. You don't," she added confidentially, "sleep quite as well as you used to when you get to be my age."

"My Mom has the same problem. She's up by six and washing the kitchen floor or baking something."

"Well, I can't say I'm that ambitious. I have this heart condition," she added, touching her bony breast. "It's a terrible nuisance. I'd never let the place deteriorate like this if I had my health. Cath-a-leen helps out on weekends, but there's only so much one person can do."

"She's a great girl."

"Oh, good as gold. Believe me, good as gold. I don't know what I'd do without her. You know," she said, dropping her voice as if to prevent any nosy neighbor from overhearing, "what the government sends me wouldn't even pay the rent."

Charlie shook his head sympathetically.

"My only worry is Billy, to tell you the truth. If he was squared away—you know, on the Force like yourself or had a good job on

Wall Street—I wouldn't care what happened to me. I've lived long enough," she concluded with a stage sigh.

"I wouldn't give up on him yet, Mrs. C.," Charlie said, although the idea of Billy becoming a cop gave him pause. "My brother Kenny was a late starter. He didn't look like he would make anything of himself for the longest time. Now he's married and raising a family over in Jersey."

"Is that right?" she said, brightening. "In Jersey, you say?"

"Big beautiful house. Swimming pool. The works. Cynthia and I go over there with my Mom just about every Sunday for dinner."

"Isn't that grand! I always wanted to move to Jersey. But my husband said the quiet would drive him crazy."

Charlie laughed. "Well, it's sure a lot more peaceful than Brooklyn."

"Isn't that lovely. Jersey! How nice for your mother."

She sat smiling as if she could see the rolling green lawn, and didn't notice at first that her guest was getting to his feet. Then she asked, "Won't you have a piece of cake? I'm sorry I never got around to offer you some."

"Thanks, Mrs. C., but I got to get home. Cynthia gets a little nervous if I stay away too long, being she's expecting and all."

"Of course. I understand perfectly. Well, I'm so glad you came by, Charlie, and I'll tell Billy you were here. Would you like him to give you a call?"

"I go back on the four-to-midnight this week. Maybe I'll give him a buzz myself if that's alright with you."

"He'll be delighted to hear from you. And give my best to your mother."

"I will, Mrs. C."


As soon as it was dark Billy took the long way around and entered the park at the less-used 10th Avenue entrance. He kept to the wooded area behind the baseball diamonds, all of which were deserted except for a couple dog owners and a flock of seagulls camped in the outfields. He made a big loop around the small lake where his father used to take him for paddleboat rides but was now full of beer cans and hamburger wrappers. A dirt trail led to higher ground, then branched out into several smaller paths, one of which continued north to Monument Hill. Park Rangers only came to this part of the park on horse-back. His pulse was beating fast—not the pleasant thrill of imminent danger he felt when he was stepping into someone's apartment to relieve them of their valuables but a raw fear that kept him short of breath and queasy in the stomach.

"Let's get this over with," he said to no one.

A rustle in the dead leaves made him start. He knew it was only a squirrel or rat—rats came out in droves at night to feast on the garbage people left behind—but the sound made his heart pound like a bass drum. He could barely make out the outline of the big tree lying like a stricken giant at the crest of the hill, its great root system indecently exposed by the bolt of lightning that had felled it. He touched the soil near the roots and found it soft. Had he approached the tree from this side last night he would have had no trouble digging a hole.

He felt the ground on the opposite side of the tree, but it seemed uniformly compact. He went back over the same area more slowly, still without success.

There was another rustle in the nearby bushes—too big a disturbance to be caused by a rat. He stared hard into the underbrush but could see nothing in the tangle of decaying foliage.

"Who's there?"

When he was younger and used to venture into these parts after dark, he was afraid of running into some kind of creature which didn't dare show its face by the light of day. His friends told stories about a monster that hid in a cave by day and came out after dark to scavenge animal and human flesh. He used to make fun of their monster but was actually just as afraid as they were.

"I said, who's there?" he called, trying to put authority in his voice.

He was answered by more rustling noises accompanied by a low but not unfriendly growl.

"Jesus. Go away. I got enough troubles."

As if understanding exactly what Billy had said, a thin dog emerged from the bushes, cautiously wagging its tail and looking up at him with timid delight.

"Just what I need."

The dog's tail moved more vigorously. It sidestepped closer until its dirty coat was flush against his leg. Billy reached down and stroked the matted hair behind its ears.

"Can you at least help me find the bone I buried?"

The dog wagged its tail enthusiastically.

"I buried it right...over here." He went down on one knee and pointed. "Can you dig it up?"

The dog barked. "Jesus. Don't do that. Just dig."

But the dog merely stood waving its rear end happily.

"Look, I'll show you."

He got down on his other knee and began making clawing motions. "Get the idea? Dig."

The dog obliged by scraping its paws at the hard ground.

"Not there. Over here."

But the dog only repeated its ineffectual scraping, never taking its eyes off its new friend.

"You're no better at this than I am. Okay, champ. Thanks for trying." He stood up and brushed his hands clean. "Well, I guess if I can't find it myself, maybe nobody else will either. Go back where you came from. Go on, scat."

He climbed over the exposed roots, having decided to risk an open trek across the field he had crossed in the mist last night. He started down the hill, not realizing until he almost reached the bottom and saw something streak by him that the dog had followed. He waved his arm menacingly, but the dog took the gesture as an invitation to play and began running hard circles around him, barking happily.

"Shh," he said, inviting the dog to come and be petted. "You gotta be quiet, boy. You'll get us both thrown in the slammer."

But as soon as he stopped petting, the dog broke into another series of circles. Billy picked up a stick and threw it at the animal. The dog retrieved it and dropped it at his feet, then lay there panting. Billy threw the stick again and the dog retrieved it. They made their way across the field in this fashion until they reached the low hill opposite the duck pond, where he had spent the previous night.

The cloud cover afforded little light except what was reflected by the city on the overcast. He could barely make out the shapes of trees. Even when he reached the top of the hill he was not certain whether the dark mass he saw was the bivouac of the homeless woman or just a pile of garbage the park attendants had not yet picked up.

The dog began sniffing at the mound of coats and rags, then gave a loud bark.

"Quiet, boy. It's okay."

There was no movement from the pile.

"Anybody home?"

The pile moved. A length of black hair appeared.

"Sorry to bother you. It's me again. Just thought I'd stop by and say hello."

The dog had kept its distance until now. But Billy's conversational tone gave it the courage to give the stack of coats a more careful examination. The woman's eyes darted toward it.

"Don't worry. He's friendly. Just a stray that seems to live here in the park. He latched onto me, and I can't seem to get rid of him. I guess he's homeless himself."

For a moment nobody spoke. Then, through the muffle of old clothes he heard, "What you want?"

"I don't want nothing. Like I said, I just thought I'd stop by and see how you was doing. I appreciate your letting me borrow the coat last night. Otherwise I'd of freezed my ass off."

There was no answer. He decided she was either out-and-out crazy or so paranoid from living alone that there was no chance of holding a real conversation with her. He was about to say goodbye when she twisted her head free of her cocoon and said, "You slept by that tree there."

"That's right. I got up early. I didn't get a chance to thank you for the coat."

"That's okay."

Well, I gotta be going." He started to turn away, then said, "Say, could I interest you in a cup of coffee?"

He had meant his question as an invitation to walk down to 7th Avenue with him. But when she replied, "Sure. Two sugars, no cream," he realized she thought he would fetch the coffee and bring it back. He had not meant to linger in the park any longer than was necessary.

"Gotcha. Be back in two shakes."

He borrowed a length of rope from the woman's shopping cart and tied the dog up to a nearby tree.

"Stay," he said, ignoring the pleading look in the animal's eyes.

He recognized no one in the luncheonette at 8th Avenue and 9th Street, not even the counterman, which was all to the good. He ordered two coffees and a cheese danish to go. Then he headed back toward the park. It was just past 7:00, with plenty of commuters still on the streets.

When he spotted a blue uniform near the Lafayette Memorial guarding the 9th Street entrance, he turned back to 8th Avenue, then walked south to 12th Street and doubled back toward the park. But the cop had walked south as well and was now standing at the entrance to the 11th Street playground.

"Where you been, man? You know, I been looking high and low for you?"

"I went to visit Brother Timothy."

"At Dodge? What for?"

"I felt a need for spiritual counseling."

"Gimme a break, Billy. When's the last time you was even to confession?"

"I confess daily. I'm my own confessor. And I give stiff penances."

"The only thing you give stiff is your dick, and that mostly goes to Rosemary Grady."

"I do not deny the sacrament to anyone."

He was lying on Brendan's sofa bed, sipping a beer and watching the ten o'clock news. He had let himself in with his own key, napped briefly, ate the danish and some stale doughnuts out of Brendan's almost empty refrigerator and drank the two coffees he had bought. He intended putting off going home as long as he dared, but not more than another half-hour—Cathleen went to bed early.

"I told you before, man, Charlie Madigan was nosing around in Scully's."

"So you did. Has anybody else been asking for me?"

"Like who?"

"Like anyone."

"Like Tommy McCready, for instance?"

"Sure, why not."

"You didn't happen to see Tommy yourself last night?"

"I might and I might not."

"If Tommy was in on that party, they're gonna be looking up and down for anybody was with him. The mayor says he wants the perpetrators brought to justice."

"Over some coon got his brains blown out?"

"It's one of them 'bias' crimes. It's supposed to count more because the victim was a nigger and the ones shot him was white."

"The yam is just as dead either way."

"That's the way I see it. But with all these black-on-white and white-on-black crimes, they're gonna make something special out it. Charlie works out of that precinct, you now, the one where the shooting took place."

"That right?"

"He thinks he's a regular Sherlock Holmes. You shoulda seen him. Hey, you remember the time we took his pants off and left him in the girls' bathroom?"

Billy hadn't thought about that incident in years. But the memory of Charlie's terror-stricken, tear-drenched face as he stood bare-bottomed in the girls' toilet where he would have to remain until someone rescued him, made him double up with mirth despite everything he had been through in the last twenty-four hours.

"You remember the look on Sister Benjy's face when Mary Sheehan told her he was in there with no pants on?"

When they calmed down Brendan said, "Level with me, Billy Boy. You know anything about that business in Flatbush?"

Billy kept his eyes on the TV screen where the newsreader was just working his way into an update on that very story.

"...in the matter of the black youth who was slain early this morning by five still-unidentified whites. Police say they have a good lead on the owner of the car. The matter has been referred to the special bias-related crime unit which the mayor instituted last year. A spokesperson for the Department says the police expect to have a breakthrough within the next few days. We'll keep you posted. Donna?"

"You see? I told you they was making a federal case out of it."

"Not quite."

"Billy, I'm telling you as your friend: If you know anything about that scam, you better tell me. Otherwise, how will I know what to say if Charlie starts nosing around again?"

"You'll say nothing, that's what. The less I tell you, the less you have to tell anyone. You wouldn't, by any chance, be thinking about your own ass, Brendan, me boy? Like maybe that jewelry you been off-loading on our friend over in Red Hook?"

"Louie wouldn't say nothing. Anyways, why would the cops question a fence like him?"

"You never know who they're gonna question in a case like this. It's a political thing. They don't give a shit about no spade getting snuffed. Niggers get shot every day of the week and twice on Sunday. If we didn't have one sitting over in City Hall right now, nobody'd give this hit a second thought."

"You still ain't answered my question: What d'you want me to say to Charlie?"

Billy sat up and glared at him.

"You say nothing. You say what you know—which is sweet piss-all. I was with Rosemary last night.... No, better yet, I was right here."

"So, you *was* with Tommy."

"I was here! You got that?"

"Yeah, I got it," Brendan said, exiting the room in search of a beer and maybe something stronger. "I got it good."

# CHAPTER EIGHT

His next stop was his mother's apartment to shower and change clothes.

"Charlie Madigan came by this morning," she said as he toweled off in the small bathroom next to the kitchen. "He's such a lovely young man. I don't know why you don't make friends with a boy like that instead of those people you do hang out with. His wife is going to have a baby."

"Did he say what he wanted?"

"Just to strike up old acquaintance. I think he's fond of you, Billy. And here you don't even bother to keep up a relationship with him."

"Did he leave a message?"

"Nothing in particular," she replied from her chair at the kitchen table. "Just to give him a call when you get the chance. Why don't you do that, Billy? Maybe he could even help find you a job."

"I will, Ma," he said, pulling on the clean underwear she had handed him even before he finished drying off. "First chance I get. But as a matter of fact I have a very important appointment this afternoon, so I'm in a bit of a hurry."

"You won't be home for dinner?"

"Afraid not."

He found a clean, ironed shirt hanging from the back of the kitchen chair. He pulled it on and began buttoning it.

"You should get a haircut, Billy. It's starting to grow wild. You need to keep up your appearance if you want to get a good job. Appearances count for a great deal."

"I will, Mom. Just as soon as I get the chance. But like I said, I'm in a hurry. Be a sweetheart and find my new sneakers."

"Sneakers? Do you think it's a good idea to go to an interview in sneakers? Why don't you wear those nice dress shoes I got you at Thom McCan's?"

"Sneakers'll do just fine for this interview. I ain't got a lot of time, though, so be a honey and do what I ask."

She pulled herself out of the old kitchen chair and secured the flimsy housecoat across her chest.

"I don't know what you'll do when you don't have me to wait on you anymore," she said only half-complainingly. "Sometimes I think that's all that keeps me going."

"We'll talk about it some other time."

"With you and your sister it's always rush, rush. I swear, I don't know how I ever bore the likes of you two."

"If Charlie calls back, tell him I went on a job interview. You don't know when I'll be back."

His hair still wet from the shower, he hurried westward down 16th Street. You rarely saw a police car on that block except in the summer when one passed through religiously every night at ten o'clock. Even so, he kept an eye out. Sure enough, he spotted a blue-and-white patrol car double-parked near 7th Avenue. He ducked into the nearest areaway until he was satisfied it was empty, then hurried on past.

"I ain't seen Tommy all week," the meth-head who was his usual source of amphetamines told him when he reached the OTB on Fifth Avenue. "I'll tell him you're looking for him."

"Don't bother. Tell him to get in touch with Brendan McCauley. Tell him Brendan has some good stuff."

"'Get in touch with Brendan.' Got it." The old junkie gave the thumbs-up sign. But Billy didn't trust him any further than he could throw a Benzedrine. For all he knew, Tommy was sitting in a station house right now, getting his brains picked.

He bought a few extra ups with the carfare his mother had given him, then stopped by a newsstand to pick up a Snickers bar, which would have to serve as lunch. The headline of the *Post* caught his eye: "ARREST IN BROOKLYN BIAS SHOOTING." He opened the paper—on an ordinary day he simply would have stolen it—and read the story. It didn't name any names, merely stated a white male had been apprehended in the Sunset Park section of Brooklyn and further arrests were anticipated. It was only a matter of time before some boys in blue—real cops, not that snotnose Charlie Madigan—would be around to question him.

He paid for the Snickers and headed toward the subway with no particular destination in mind. If the cops nailed him now, the best deal he could hope for was an accessory charge, which he could probably plea-bargain to attempted manslaughter or some other less serious felony. He had already had a taste of jail a few years back after he threw a garbage can through a store window on 9th Avenue when the owner refused to advance him a six pack on credit. As a result, he had spent a few days in the Brooklyn House of Detention and found the conditions there appalling. He hated to think what doing real time would be like.

The subway was virtually empty. He doubted the Transit Police had his description, but he decided to make like a homeless person just in case, turning up the collar of his jacket to hide his face.

The train made a few stops in downtown Brooklyn, then passed under the East River and came up in Manhattan. When it reached Greenwich Village he got off.

The Village, especially the area around Washington Square Park, was one of the few parts of the city outside Brooklyn he was familiar with. He had been venturing into the Village since his early teens to cop grass. He had also done a bit of fag-bashing before AIDS made homosexuals off-limits even to a closed fist. He was familiar with the basketball courts on 6th Avenue and all the head shops along 8th Street. Just two weeks ago he had copped from a Jamaican with dreadlocks down to his knees. The dope turned out to be garbage, but he hadn't felt inclined to ask for his money back.

The park itself was patrolled regularly, both by uniformed and plainclothes police—not that they put any noticeable crimp in the drug trade. Joggers loped around the park's perimeter all day and far into the night. Inside, young mothers and nannies supervised their charges in fenced-off playgrounds. Africans attending NYU played soccer on the grass. In the big circular pool, dry now, street musicians were entertaining a thin afternoon crowd, while at the southwestern corner some old white men were playing chess with young blacks on concrete tables.

It looked like a peaceful urban scene, but to Billy's eye there was an undercurrent of activity not obvious to the French and Japanese tourists taking snapshots under the big victory arch. The real dealers—not all of them in drugs—were scattered throughout the park, on benches where old folks were reading newspapers and tired shoppers watching the Africans lope across their makeshift soccer field. Pimps and purveyors of all sorts of ill-gotten goods from hot stereos to illegal abortion pills, they might have been aliens let down from a space ship and only visible to the eyes of other aliens.

As he ambled past the statue of Garibaldi, he spotted a well-dressed young man he happened to know was a dealer in prepubescent boys. A glint of recognition passed between them. He felt in his pocket to check that his supply of ups was safe. No one would bother him here, certainly none of the sappy cops. There were dozens of young men just like himself, most in need of a bath, many deliberately cultivating the look on fat bank accounts. The real down-and-out were picking through trash baskets for redeemable soda cans and pizza crusts.

He sat down and watched some kids do tricks on skateboards, weaving in and out of the pedestrian traffic like birds darting through tree branches. He needed a place to spend the night. He was friendly with a couple dealers in the East Village, but they were as apt to draw the attention of police as he was. Spending the night on the subway, his only other option, was risky but not as bad as going back to his own neighborhood. He hated sleeping on the trains. He did it once when his sister convinced his mother to lock him out of the house. That night he was accosted twice by perverts who waved their wangers at him until he scared them off with one of his crazy routines, but he had sore knees for a week, thanks to the knocking they got from the clubs of Transit cops.

He was weighing these alternatives when a young woman sat down on the bench beside him. In his experience, a young woman didn't sit down next to you if she didn't want to make friends.

"Ever try that?" he said, nodding at the skateboarders decked out in black and orange Spandex.

"Skiing's my thing."

"That right?" He sat up and took a closer look. She had on tattered dungarees but was wearing a hundred-dollar sweater. "Where do you ski?"

"The Poconos. Vermont. When I can swing it. My parents are real jerks about money. They're afraid to send me any. They think I'll spend it on drugs."

"Do you?" he asked with his most engaging smile.

"Well," she giggled, "just a teensy weensy."

"Say, didn't I see you in Eco class?" he said, using a line he just overheard from a neighboring bench.

"No, I'm an anthropology major."

"Is that right? My mother's an anthropologist."

"No fooling?"

"Well, I should say used to be. She's retired now. After my father died she sort of lost interest, if you know what I mean."

"Did she go on any big digs?"

He seemed to consider the question seriously for a few moments, then said, "Two or three."

"Wow! That's what I'd like to do. You know, where you find some ancient king's tomb or something. We get to go to Mexico the summer of our junior year."

"You're a sophomore?"

"Freshman," she admitted.

"From around these parts?"

"Old Westbury. Know where that is?"

"More or less."

He didn't, but it sounded like "Old Money."

"Real Boresville. I mean, you can't even get a good joint. And the cops watch every move you make."

"No shit?"

"A real drag."

"I'll bet you don't have that problem here in the Village."

"Are you kidding? I could buy a kilo of coke not two blocks from here."

"Is that what you're into, coke?"

She scrunched up her nose in a way that made her look like she was nine years old.

"Nah, I like smack."

"Heroin?"

"Ssh!" She looked around cautiously. "This place is full of cops in plainclothes."

"Geez, I'm glad you told me."

"Listen, I got some good grass in my room. You want a taste?"

"Well," he said, himself checking for the undercover cops he could spot as easily as if they were wearing sandwich boards, "I really should be getting back to the library. I got this here term paper due in the morning."

"Just a quick hit," she coaxed. "Besides, the library's open all night."

"That's true," he said. "Well, you talked me into it."

The girl, whose name was Melissa, took him to a dorm on University Place. Her room overlooked the park.

"Great place for a sniper," he said.

"Sniper? You're funny."

He turned away from the window and found there was a second girl in the room. He used to have fantasies about going away to college, before it became obvious that the great achievement of his life would be getting a high school diploma. He pictured himself on a rural campus in New England, someplace full of quadrangles and gothic architecture. There would be horseback riding, polo and archery and all sorts of activities he had only seen in movies but which he imagined college boys took for granted.

He had popped one of his ups on the elevator and was feeling pretty perky. Ups made him horny. But he had decided to stay on his best behavior. With a little luck, he might get invited to spend the night.

"Billy, this is Jeannie."

"Hi, Jeannie," he said, not sure if a handshake, a high-five or just a cool wave was in order. "Jeannie's my very best friend. We do everything together."

"Ev-ery-thing?" Jeannie drawled, making Melissa frown, then break into a bout of giggles. He felt like he was at a pajama party.

"Anyway, Jeannie always has the best dope, don't you Jeannie? Anytime I want to cop, I just go to Jeannie's room and she gives me whatever I want."

"No shit—I mean, no kidding," he said. "I could introduce you to a few new customers if you like, Jeannie."

A plump, homely brunette, Jeannie said, "Thanks, but it's strictly recreational for me. I just share what I have with friends."

"So, what did you bring us?" Melissa said, closing the door.

69

Jeannie fished into the pocket of the heavy cardigan she was wearing.

"One, two, three joints. The guy who sold them said they were Jamaican Gold."

"Alright!" Melissa said. "Who's got a match?"

Billy obliged, then sat down on Melissa's bed. Jeannie sat down in an orange desk chair. She lit up, then passed the joint to Melissa who inhaled deeply and held her breath with a look that reminded Billy of a kid trying not to pee in her pants. He took the third hit and passed the joint back to Jeannie.

They repeated this procedure several times, but Billy was still waiting to feel something.

Not so the girls. The smoke had scarcely entered their lungs when they began saying, "Oh, wow," and "This is really good shit."

"I feel like I'm floating," Melissa said, her eyes glassy.

"Me too. God, pot makes me sooo horny."

He was about to inform them they had been sold garbage, but decided to hold off a little longer.

"How do you feel, Billy?"

"Yeah, the same way."

Melissa said, "Go check the door, Jeannie." She looked like she had swallowed half a dozen barbiturates. "Say, Billy Boy, you ever get blowed by two girls at the same time?"

It was rush hour when he left the dorm. All he had in his pockets was two singles, a couple quarters and a token. He would need the token to get back to Brooklyn—or to get somewhere. He still had no place to stay.

There was a bank of public telephones at the southern perimeter of the park. He dropped a quarter into one and dialed Brendan McCauley's number. He let it ring half a dozen times, then hung up.

The phone failed to return his quarter.

"Damn."

He was down to his last twenty-five cents. He dialed a Manhattan number.

"Miss Conover, please."

When the voice on the other end asked who she should say was calling, he replied "Mory Barthfeld."

"Hold on, Mr. Barthfeld. I'll see if I can locate Miss Conover for you."

Half a minute later his sister came on the line.

"Hello? Who is this, please?"

"The fucking Dalai Lama. Who did you think it was?"

"What do you want? I'm in the middle of a conference."

"Well, I'm sorry to interrupt your important conference, but I need to meet you after work."

"What for? Why can't it wait till I get home?"

"Because why is a crooked letter. I'll meet you outside your office in half an hour."

"If it's money you want, forget it. I'm not giving you a penny."

"Who said anything about money? We're talking a matter of life and death here, Sis. Would I take you out of an important conference just for money?"

"What is this about? Is Ma alright?"

"She was fine when I saw her this morning."

"Have you done something wrong? Are the police after you? I knew this would happen some day."

"It must be wonderful to have the gift of prophecy."

"If you got yourself into hot water, you can just get yourself out again."

"That's not a very sisterly attitude, Cath-a-leen. Besides, if you don't help me, I'll have to bring my problem home to Mom, and you know how that will upset her."

"What kind of trouble are you in?"

"I ain't done nothing. Only, I'm not sure New York's Finest will see it that way."

"I knew this was coming. I just knew it."

"So, you'll meet me on Broadway in half an hour?"

"No, not outside my building."

"You don't want to be seen with me?"

"Exactly. Meet me...on Church Street. Across from the World Trade Center. By the cemetery."

"That seems an appropriate spot."

"But I can't get out of here for another forty-five minutes."

"I'll wait for you."

He walked down West Broadway past the storefront art galleries and restaurants, taking his time. His denim jacket gave little protection against the cold wind whipping off the Hudson, but he knew Cathleen would be on time. Cathleen was never late.

His usual view of her was in baggy jeans and an old work shirt, pushing a vacuum cleaner across the worn living room rug or throwing something together on the stove for the three of them to eat. But this evening he saw walking toward him an attractive woman in a tailored cloth coat and long shiny hair. It was hard to believe this was the same girl whose pigtails he used to pull mercilessly, the skinny teenager whose boyfriends he mocked until she cried.

"Let's get this over with as quick as possible. I still don't understand why it couldn't wait till I got home."

"The truth is, I'm a little short of funds. That's where I was thinking maybe you could help me out."

"You do want money! I ought to have my head examined. Well, you're not getting anything from me. Go bum a few dollars off your junkie friends. This well's run dry."

"No, no," he said, his tone plaintive. "It ain't like that, Cath-a-leen. I ain't used no drugs in a dog's age, honest. I got other things on my mind—problems, big problems."

"Like what?"

He looked around like a movie character checking to see if any spies were about.

"I was kind of in the wrong place at the wrong time."

"So the police really are looking for you."

"Not exactly. At least, I hope not. Let's just say it'd be safer for me to stay out of the neighborhood until the real culprits are apprehended."

She clapped her hand to her mouth. "You got involved in something serious!"

"No. Honest to God. On Daddy's grave."

"Don't bring Daddy into it. Don't even mention his name," she said, looking like she meant it.

"I'm sorry. I really am. I just meant that as God is my judge I didn't do nothing."

"Then why are the police looking for you?"

"I told you, I don't know they are. I just want to lay low until things blow over."

"Ma said Charlie Madigan came around."

"I heard."

"Did his visit have anything to do with this business they want you for?"

"I don't think so. I don't know. Listen, you gotta trust me. I wouldn't lie to you about something like this. I just need a few dollars so's I can get something to eat."

"If you don't come home the police will be even more suspicious."

"Maybe so. But those guys don't treat you so nice down the station house. Even when they know you didn't do nothing. They try to get you to tell them something about your friends."

"So, it was your friends did it."

"No. I mean, I don't know."

"You're afraid if you tell the cops something, your friends'll take it out of your hide. It's your friends you're hiding from, right? Not the cops?"

"Look, just give me a few dollars and I promise you everything'll be alright."

"Why don't you ask Brendan for a loan? Isn't he your buddy?"

"I can't."

"Why not? Is Brendan one of the people the police are looking for?"

He said nothing, allowing her to believe he was acting out of loyalty. Meanwhile, some passersby took note of the pretty, well-dressed woman talking to the disheveled but remarkably handsome young man.

She abruptly opened her pocketbook and pulled out a ten-dollar bill.

"If the cops or whoever do catch up with you, don't bother calling home."

"I won't. I won't bother you again. I swear."

She stared hard at him, too exasperated to point out that they both knew he was lying. Then she walked briskly away as if he were nothing more to her than a beggar she had handed a quarter.

# CHAPTER NINE

He tried Brendan's number again, but there was still no answer. Then he headed toward the subway, more to get warm than with any real destination in mind. Near the entrance was a newsstand displaying the late edition of the *Post*. "BREAKTHROUGH IN FLATBUSH SLAYING." He picked up a copy and turned to page three. "A police spokesperson today said the Department expected to make arrests soon in the case of the black youth who was slain early yesterday morning on Flatbush Avenue in Brooklyn. The identity of the car the killer was driving has been obtained through a license number one of the dead youth's friends gave to police.

"The Mayor expressed satisfaction with the progress of the case. He said at an afternoon press conference that bias crimes of this sort cannot be tolerated and will be prosecuted to the full extent of the law.

"The victim, Andrew Mott, was pronounced dead at the scene by a team of medical emergency personnel. Mr. Mott was a youth worker in the Flatbush area, employed by a local community center. At the time of the slaying he was trying to dissuade members of a local gang from hanging out on a street corner."

"This ain't no reading room, sonny," the newsstand vendor said.

"Yeah, yeah," Billy replied, putting the newspaper back on the pile. "Merry Christmas to you too."

There was no question now of returning to 16th Street. He would have to spend the night in the park again.

When the subway arrived in Park Slope he followed the crowd toward the 8th Avenue exit. Most turned down the avenue, leaving the remainder to trudge up the hill toward the expensive sandstones along

74

9th Street and the big apartment houses and co-ops facing the park. There was no sign of the police, though when he reached Prospect Park West he could make out a patrol car at Bartel-Pritchard Square several blocks to the south, a favorite spot for making monthly traffic-ticket quotas.

Once inside the park he kept close to the trees and bushes near the new bandshell that drew big crowds on summer weekends. Some teens were using the swings in the playground, but they paid no attention to him.

Evening traffic was careening down the park drive, moving in clumps of twenty or thirty cars, then leaving a long gap until the next bunch appeared. He ran across it and turned north toward the Tennis House, trying to stay in the shadows. Once past the Tennis House the park suddenly became much darker, the path lights having been broken by vandals or allowed to go dark from lack of maintenance. He was only a few yards from the hill where the homeless woman was camped out, but he could barely see ten feet in front of him. A bag he had carried all the way from Manhattan was wet with the spillover from the container of coffee it held.

He mouthed a silent prayer to the God he no longer believed in that the woman would still be there. When he was a few yards from her tree, he finally was able to make out the cocoon of rags and old coats. But even before he had a chance to congratulate himself, he felt something slam into his leg and a moment later realized it had bitten him.

"Jesus Christ!"

The dog started to bark, then backed off and stood between himself and the homeless woman, snarling.

"You want to call off this beast? He's already eaten half my leg."

For a moment, he was afraid he would have to limp away and take his chances with the police. But then he heard the woman say, "Stay, Snoopy. Stay!"

The dog sniffed him thoroughly from a distance, then walked back to the woman's tree and lay down.

"That the same mutt followed me here last night?"

"That's him," she said, her head visible now. He decided she must be schizo, okay one day and snapping at you the next. He thanked God today was her good day.

"Snoop's my buddy now. Nobody would dare come close with him here. I can't afford to buy him food. I just give him whatever I find in the trash. He doesn't seem to mind."

Billy wondered what it was that she subsisted on herself. Then he remembered the soggy bag he was holding and handed her the tepid coffee.

"Better late than never."

"What's this?"

"The coffee you wanted. Two sugars, no milk."

"You had it with you all this time?"

"Not exactly. I kind of got delayed."

A long dark hand emerged from the shell. The arm attached to it seemed thinner than a broom handle.

"It might be a little cold. I picked it up in Manhattan."

The coffee smell started his stomach rumbling. He realized he should have tried to scare up some food too. But he didn't dare venture into the streets again before morning rush hour.

"It's good," she said, taking several quick sips. "Want some?"

He took a polite taste.

She gave him a warm overcoat and let him sit down beside her. The dog lay a few feet away, one ear turned toward their conversation, the other to a variety of night sounds in the park.

"Your leg okay?" she asked.

"More or less."

"Where will you sleep tonight?"

"I thought maybe I'd try the Waldorf. Actually, the last time I stayed there I didn't like the class of people they let in."

She laughed. It was a light, tinkly laugh that reminded him of girls he used to meet at high school mixers—foolish virgins so oversexed they could barely stand still.

"Of course, I could accept the invitation from the Mayor to spend a couple days at Gracie Mansion. But I always forget which way the bathroom is when I get up to pee during the night."

She laughed again.

"Then again, Prospect Park ain't so bad this time of year."

"Sleep here? Why? You have a home, don't you?"

"After a fashion. Actually, I'm kind of persona non grateful at the moment."

"Non 'grata,'" she said. "Persona non grata."

"That's what I said. Anyway, my sister would just as soon I don't show my face for a while."

For a while he sat listening to the ducks call to each other as they settled down on the big pond. They at least didn't have to worry about where they would sleep tonight.

"You could stay here if you like. I can let you have another coat."

"Thanks," he said. "I appreciate it."

"I had a friend named Conover."

"Is that so? What was their first name?"

"Shawnee."

"That wouldn't be my sister, then. Her name is Cath-a-leen."

"I meant back where I come from."

"Where might that be?"

For a moment he thought he had asked a more personal question than it seemed. But then she said, "The Midwest."

"Ah, yes. That's on the other side of the Hudson. You sleep here every night?"

"Why do you want to know that?"

"Just curious."

"This is my private place," she said, not in a friendly tone. "I don't want nobody else to find out about it."

"My lips are sealed."

"You wouldn't be my friend no more. I mean it."

"Relax. No one knows I'm here, and I don't intend on telling nobody."

"I'm not going back to that shelter. I'd rather die. If they find me here, they'll make me go back to the shelter."

"It's pretty bad there?"

She shrunk further inside her cocoon like a turtle drawing into its shell. "People bother you."

He could only guess what she meant, but the possibilities all seemed unpleasant.

"It must get pretty lonely in the park, though. Do you stay here all the time?"

"I go for walks. Sometimes I go down to the library. I can't be away too long, 'cause someone might take my spot."

"How do you survive? Moneywise, if you don't mind my asking."

"I manage."

He listened to the ducks and began to feel sleepy. He was starting to drift off when he heard her say, "If you try anything they can hear me scream, you know."

"Who?"

"The Park people. The police."

He doubted anyone but another homeless person could hear anything that went on in the park late at night, but he assured her his intentions were honorable.

Then, her voice heavily muffled, she said, "If you get chilly, you can take another coat."

He dozed off and dreamed he was a kid again, sleigh-riding on Monument Hill. You had to wait your turn in a long line at the top, but you went like greased lightening if the slope was packed hard or icy. More than one kid ended up with a broken limb when he ran into a tree or snow bank. Amazingly, he never suffered anything but minor scratches and bruises although, true to his image, he took wild risks.

In his dream, the snow was fresh and hard-packed. He had nothing on his mind but the thrill that lay ahead until, waiting his turn behind some older boys, he remembered the murder weapon he had buried just a few yards away. To add to his confusion, he spotted Charlie Madigan in line behind him, not the wimpy snotnose whose mittens he used to snatch, but an armed ten-year-old cop.

It was his turn to launch his sleigh down the icy slope. But Charlie was watching with that cold, sadistic cop look that seemed to say he was just waiting for Billy to make a false move.

He looked for the shortest route to the hill's bottom, slammed his body onto the hard snow and flew down the slope.

Steering was impossible. Ahead was the Needle, two trees between which he must somehow guide the rocketing sled. As the trees came closer and the space between them barely seemed to widen, he began to recite the Act of Contrition. But there was little likelihood he could avoid hellfire after a life of petty crime and gross sexual misconduct. Hot tears of self-pity stung his eyes and immediately turned to ice. There were just a few yards left between himself and the trees, which were moving closer together like perverse cartoon animations instead of farther apart as they should have.

"It's okay," he heard a far-away voice say. "It's alright."

He awoke trembling, his heart pounding. For a moment, he felt a surge of relief. But then he remembered the dream was true and in real life Charlie Madigan really was out to get him.

He started to cry. He tried to be quiet about it, but his hopelessness broke through his attempts at restraint.

He felt a warm hand on his own. Through a blur of tears, he saw the homeless woman sitting upright beside him. She was far from attractive, but her eyes were big and full of compassion, the kind of eyes that could get a girl into trouble. "I sometimes get nightmares too."

He didn't dare speak for fear of sobbing again.

"You want some more coats to warm you up?"

He shook his head. But she pulled a couple more rags off the pile and wrapped them around him. The smell was vile but their bulk felt good.

"That's better," she said, then slipped back into her mound like some kind of shellfish that only leaves briefly to feed or mate.

# CHAPTER TEN

The day dawned bright and sunny. Billy loved sunny mornings. He got a high from them, just as he became gloomy when he awoke to overcast or rain. His bad dream seemed far away. He still got a sinking feeling in his stomach when he thought about the gun. But he felt more confident that it would not be found or, if it was, no one could trace it back to him. After all, it was not he who pulled the trigger on that hapless black kid. He was guilty of nothing more than being foolish enough to be there at the time. And he couldn't have just walked away at one o'clock in the morning in the middle of a black neighborhood.

He decided to risk going to the luncheonette on 9th Street to bring back breakfast for himself and the homeless woman. She liked the idea, and in the bright morning light he liked the way she looked, ragged but vulnerable and even pretty in a rough way. He said he would be back shortly and set off humming an old hymn.

He crossed the park drive and headed toward the children's playground where a few earlybirds were already making mud cakes in the sandbox. His mother used to take him to the old playground that stood on this same site. The facilities were cruder then, but he wouldn't trade these brightly colored geometries for the old monkey bars he used to hang from by his heels while his mother wept with anxiety. Even so, he enjoyed the sounds of the kids at play and began to whistle something catchier than the tune he had started out with.

Thanks to the good weather, there were more than the usual number of people on the streets—joggers padding the sidewalk outside the park and an army of commuters heading toward the 7th Avenue subway station.

He hadn't had a real meal in almost twenty-four hours, and even though the ups he took had suppressed his appetite, it came back this morning with a vengeance. He could smell the coffee half a long block away. His hunger distracted him from the dull brown sedan double-parked part way down the block as if looking for a parking space or waiting to pick up someone from a nearby sandstone. But when it began to move with him and then to keep pace, he darted a glance inside and saw two young men in the kind of light jackets favored by plainclothes police. He cursed his stupidity for not noticing them in time but managed a weak smile and nod at the one watching him from behind a partially rolled-down window.

"Morning. Beautiful morning, ain't it."

The cop said nothing. The car continued to move at a steady pace with his own.

"Hold it right there."

For a second his legs ached to run. It was all he could do to resist the urge, judging—correctly—that the cop would be reaching for his gun as soon as the door of the car opened.

"Assume the position."

Billy spread his hands across the car's roof and did the same with his legs on the black macadam.

"Is there some sort of problem, Officer? Are you looking for some-one in particular? Maybe I can help you."

"You can help alright," the young cop replied, "by keeping your fucking mouth shut. What's your name?"

"Dwight," Billy said. "Dwight Harrington."

"Where do you live, Dwight?"

"Well, actually, I'm temporarily without an address right now."

"Is that right?"

"Unfortunately."

"What do you think, Marty?" the cop said to his partner. Billy was pretty sure neither recognized him. But he tried to keep his face averted.

"He fits the description," the partner said. "We may as well let McCaffrey have a look at him."

"Hands behind your back," the cop ordered.

Billy hesitated only a second, but that was long enough for the cop to pull his hands off the car and jam them hard against his back-bone and clamp cuffs on his wrists. Then he opened the back door of the car and, with his hand on Billy's head, pushed him inside.

He had been arrested before, once for possession, the other time for throwing that garbage can through a plate glass window. But those had been straightforward affairs, a matter of being put into a holding cell at the station house and then released or transferred to the House of Detention on Atlantic Avenue. Neither experience had been pleasant, especially the three days in the House of D. But this was his first time in a police interrogation room. It was a plain, unwelcoming place, small and badly in need of a paint job. The cop removed the handcuffs from his wrists, but the skin was already broken. He was told to sit down and wait.

He had already decided how he would handle the interrogation. He doubted Tommy had ratted on him. No one else in that car even knew his full name, so the cops were probably on a fishing expedition.

A beefy detective entered the room carrying a file. He paid no more attention to Billy than if he were a fellow employee. He stood reading the file for the better part of a minute, then suddenly turned toward another cop standing outside the door and handed it to him.

"Billy Conover?" he said as if this were to be a job interview rather than a homicide interrogation.

"Right."

The cop eyed him sidelong. He was in his late forties and reminded Billy of his maternal uncles.

"You're sure it isn't—what was it you called yourself—Dwight?"

Billy smiled the way he did when one of his high school teachers decided to talk to him about his grades.

"A memory lapse. I hadn't had breakfast yet."

The cop smiled genially and nodded as if to say, all in good fun.

"Maybe you'd like a cup of coffee?"

"Don't mind if I do," Billy said, thinking he wouldn't mind a couple of ups to go with it.

The detective called to someone in the squad room to bring in two coffees. Then he pulled a chair away from the table, turned it around, and straddled it with his big thighs.

"Conover. You got cousins in Canarsie?"

Billy pretended to think about this for a moment, then said, "Distant."

The cop nodded, studying Billy as if scrutinizing him for signs of measles or chicken pox.

"So, what you do for a living, Billy?"

Billy was no more taken in by the man's friendly manner than he had been by the brothers', who sometimes were most on the verge of cuffing you just when they seemed to be getting chummiest. But he also couldn't help liking something about the big cop. He sensed they even had something in common apart from their Hibernian ancestry. He was making his way through life much as the cop was, pretending to be what he was not, keeping up a mask and watching his back. He had always believed he could be a cop if he wanted. But he knew he would never be able to keep his hands off the loot cops were exposed to, and he decided he'd rather be an honest thief than a crooked policeman.

"At the moment I'm temporarily unemployed."

"What sort of work do you do, Billy? I mean ordinarily."

The detective pulled a pack of cigarettes from his shirt pocket, removed one and started to raise it toward his mouth. Then he suddenly offered it to Billy. Billy didn't smoke, but he allowed the cop to light it for him.

"This and that. General clerical work—filing, light typing, that sort of thing."

The cop nodded distractedly. "It's all computerized now, I guess. I mean, there must be less and less work for somebody who doesn't know how to work those damn things."

The last time Billy saw the inside of an office was when he worked part of a summer on Wall Street. There had been plenty of computers around even then, but they didn't seem to have much to do with what went on in the mailroom.

"Actually, I'll be taking some computer courses next semester."

The cop nodded eagerly as if this were news he had been waiting to here. Then the coffees arrived. He handed one to Billy, who dumped in all three sugars and burnt his lip sipping it.

"So, at the moment," the cop went on, "the way you support yourself is...?"

Billy took another try at the hot coffee.

"I live with my mother."

"She works?"

"My sister does."

The cop did not look surprised. Billy's stomach growled for something more substantial.

The detective laid his thick arms on top of the big table, made of the same blond wood as the old school desks in Holy Family. "Just how do you spend your time these days? Say, on Monday night this week?"

Billy furrowed his brow as if Monday were a long time ago and sipped some coffee. "Geez, I dunno. Monday?" He stared up at the ceiling, scratched his head, put the coffee down on the table. "That was the night of Jinny McCormick's wake. I was at Roche's funeral parlor over on 9th Avenue. I, uh, had a little altercation with Jinny's brother, so I'm sure there are plenty of people who can vouch for my presence," he added with a boyish grin which, he noted, was reflected on the cop's own face.

"Where'd you go after the wake?"

"After?"

"Sure. The wake breaks up at what, eight-thirty, nine o'clock?"

"Let's see. I think I had a couple beers."

"At Scully's?"

"More like outside of Scully's. I'm not exactly welcome in that establishment."

"Why's that, Billy?"

"I guess it's because of a little difference of opinion I once had with a bartender in there. I guess you could say I'm 'barred' from the place."

"So where'd you go after that, Billy? We're talking maybe one, one-thirty in the morning."

"One, one-thirty? I must have been in bed. Like I told you, I'm supposed to be attending this here computer training next semester, and my mother wanted me to get up early the next morning to find out about it."

"So, you were at home from what time?"

"I dunno. Maybe midnight. Half-past."

"And you didn't leave the house for the rest of the night?"

"That's right. My mother was there. So was my sister."

The cop nodded, but he said, "The way we hear it, you weren't in your bed when your sister left for work the next morning."

Billy regarded the man mutely. How could the police know he didn't sleep at his mother's house? Cathleen would no more rat to a cop than he would himself. His mother must have told them. Charlie Madigan must have got it out of her, the silly old bitch.

"Wait, you said Monday? That's right, I went out again."

The cop nodded, but the expression on his red face was not one Billy thought he would want to meet in an alleyway when his pockets were full of someone's jewelry.

"I stayed at my friend Brendan's," he said, recalling that Rosemary had already told Charlie Madigan that she hadn't seen him in weeks. "He lives a few doors down the block."

"His full name?"

"Brendan McCauley. 4350 16th Street. Apartment three, front."

The cop wrote down this information in a small notebook.

"McCauley... McCauley... Don't I know that name?"

Billy gave him his most innocent look. "I think Brendan has a couple cousins on the Force."

"So you stayed at this Brendan character's...until when?"

"Until whenever I woke up the next morning."

"Which was about what time? A rough estimate, Billy."

"Nine. Maybe nine-thirty."

"This is Tuesday we're talking about."

"Right."

"You couldn't be mistaken, by any chance. I mean, about going to Brendan's house?"

Billy laughed discretely. "How could I forget? It was only two nights ago."

The cop smiled, but Billy was starting to think he would prefer a scowl.

"You don't mind if we check this out?"

"Naw, go ahead."

"You see, Billy, the reason we have to do that, there was a homicide that night over in Flatbush. Maybe you read about it or seen it on the TV. A shine got wasted on Flatbush Avenue."

"Now that you mention it, I did see something."

"Where'd you spend last night, Billy?"

"I was in the Village."

"Greenwich Village?"

He nodded.

"All night?"

"I stayed with a couple girls at NYU."

The cops eyebrows went up. "In the dorms?"

Billy nodded, searching the man's face hopefully for prurient interest.

"You must be quite the lady's man."

Billy shrugged. "I get my share."

The cop made a flourish of opening his notepad. "What was the name of these girls, Billy?"

Billy took a deep breath, shook his head and said, "I'm afraid I can't tell you..."

The cop looked up skeptically.

"...but one of them gives the best blowjob in Christendom."

If nothing else, he decided as he walked back up the hill from the precinct, he knew Tommy McCready hadn't finked on him. Otherwise, he wouldn't be out on the streets again. In fact, the police had actually done him a favor by bringing him in for questioning: He could go home now without fear of being rousted out of bed in the middle of the night. He could resume a normal life, minus perhaps some of his usual freelance work with Brendan. He felt like giving a little skip and clicking his heels but instead decided to celebrate in the fashion that most suited him.

As he turned the corner onto Fifth Avenue he spotted Charlie Madigan leaning against the wall of a building across from the OTB. But instead of turning away as he would have just a couple hours ago, Billy crossed the street and gave his former classmate a big wave.

"Charlie, me boy!"

The young cop regarded him with a mixture of surprise and disdain.

"Hello, Billy. Where you been keeping yourself? You been the invisible man for the past few days."

"To tell you the truth, Charlie, I've had a number of amorous appointments. One of them has the best set of lungs in the Ivy League."

Charlie frowned in confusion.

"Then, of course, I had a little chat with the boys over at the Seven

Two. About that shooting in Flatbush. Maybe you heard about it?"

"I heard."

"That's right, Flatbush is your precinct, ain't it. You been assigned to the case, by any chance?"

"Naw, that stuff's for Homicide," Charlie said, taking a quick look over his left shoulder. Cops were always looking over their shoulders, Billy had noticed. "But we're all keeping our eyes and ears open," he added with a meaningful look.

"Not a bad idea, Charlie. Not a bad idea. Is that why you're sleuthing around the OTB? Hoping to pick up a lead?"

Charlie regarded him the way he used to when Billy was about to talk him into some lamebrain prank that was likely to get them both into hot water. He had never been good at coming up with a good retort then, and he still wasn't.

"Say, Charlie, you remember the time we climbed up the church roof and hollered down the chimney during mass?"

The incident was still so vivid to the young cop, he found himself staring back not at a twenty-three-year-old Billy Conover but at the younger Billy who had talked him into sneaking up into the choir loft and then out onto the church roof. They were both altar boys but, unlike Billy, until that Sunday morning Charlie had an unblemished record. He was even one of those singled out for the priesthood and as such was given special responsibilities and privileges, such as helping take care of the chalice and other sacred vessels. The idea of his climbing onto the church roof with the likes of Billy Conover to shout down the chimney during high mass seemed just as preposterous and embarrassing now, fifteen years later, as it did at the time. As he had stood shivering on that sharply slanted roof, all of Brooklyn laid out around him from the deep blue waters of the harbor to the misty reaches of Long Island, he recalled the time Jesus was conducted by the devil to the pinnacle of some high place after his long fast in the desert. There he was offered all the kingdoms in sight if he would just kneel down and adore the Evil One. Of course, he refused.

But what was he, Charlie Madigan, honor-medal winner and apple of the nuns' eyes, doing up on that cold and windy height from which he could so easily fall, in the company of this diabolical classmate who seemed able to talk him into anything at anytime? Would he never learn how to avoid doing Billy Conover's will? Was he afraid Billy would really throw him off the roof, as he had threatened to do? Or was it because Billy had some other hold over him, some power which Jesus Christ could overcome but before which he, a mere eight-year-old mortal, was powerless?

"Yo, Earth to Charlie Madigan. I axt you, how's Cynthia and the baby?"

"Fine."

"I didn't know you was gonna be a father, Charlie. I didn't think you had it in you."

"What's that supposed to mean?"

"Nothing. Congratulations, that's all. I hope he's a nice healthy kid."

"He will be."

"Great. I hope he stays that way."

"Don't worry, he will."

"Hey, I gotta run. Big job interview. Company wants to hire me for some young-executive program. Gotta go home and put on a suit. Give my love to Cynthia."

"Yeah, sure."

"And I hope you catch them killers, Charlie. It's getting so you can't walk the streets no more."

# CHAPTER ELEVEN

Billy's next stop was Brendan's. Brendan wasn't home, but Billy availed himself of his shower as well as a fresh set of underwear, which he found neatly stacked in a bureau drawer despite the mess in the rest of the apartment. His jacket was still muddy, but he would fix that as soon as he returned home. In the meantime he intended to catch up on the sleep that had been denied him for the past couple days.

When he awoke, it was mid-afternoon. There was still no sign of Brendan. Ordinarily, the only time Brendan left the neighborhood was to deliver rent receipts to his mother in Bay Ridge. But this was only March 29th—too early to collect rent.

There was nothing in the refrigerator but a stale loaf of bread, two questionable eggs and a dark chunk of butter. He ate some bread and turned on the TV. It was too early for the news, so he watched one of the afternoon talk shows, then switched to a rival channel but found the topics—Lesbian violence against men; cross-dressing minorities—stupid. Nor was he in the mood for the pornographic videos Brendan left lying around the apartment.

He was thinking of taking a stroll around the neighborhood to get some fresh air and had already pulled on his jacket, when Brendan suddenly came through the door.

"Hello, Bren. How's tricks?"

Brendan regarded him as if he were a dead man come back to life.

"What the hell're you doing here? Where the hell've you been?"

"Here and there. I stopped by the precinct this morning, at their request of course. Something about that killing in Flatbush. I told them I couldn't be no help, but they thanked me profusely for giving them the benefit of my expertise."

"You heard they picked up Tommy McCready?"

"I assumed as much."

"You ain't told them nothing?"

"I had nothing to tell, Brendan. Like I said, I was right here with you that night."

"The hell you were."

"The hell I *was*. If I slipped out for a beer, that's nobody's business but my own."

"Says you."

"Says me. And so will you say, old friend."

Brendan emptied the contents of the plastic bag he had been carrying—a quart of milk, hamburger meat and a bottle of ketchup.

"Planning a gourmet feast, I see."

"You think I can live on what my mother pays me? The old bitch, I oughta slit her throat."

"And kill the golden goose?"

"What golden goose? You see the shit I eat? Say, when are we gonna get back to work?"

Billy walked over to the window overlooking the backs of the buildings on 15th Street. In his youth, they all housed people like the Conovers and McCauleys. Now they had gone co-op, had their facades redone, new windows installed and wooden decks built in the yards. The owners drove Volvos and RVs and had dinner parties on the decks in summertime.

"For the moment, I think it might be a good idea if I remained in semi-retirement. Just temporary. Till this Flatbush business blows over. If I get caught in somebody's bedroom right now, it could prove embarrassing."

"Man, I hope you ain't punking out."

Billy turned away from the window.

"No way. Just tryna be careful for a change."

"You? Gimme a break."

"In my old age. Don't worry, Bren. We'll be back in business same as always before the daffodils are up."

Brendan went back to putting away his meager provisions. "By that time," he said, "I'll be eating cat food."

Billy's mother seemed unconcerned by his long absence, her mind apparently on other things. She stared at him red-eyed and said, "Billy, something terrible's happened to your sister. She's been..."

His first thought was that Cathleen had been run over. That was the principle danger they had been warned against all through their childhood, and his sister had never been one for looking in both directions. But from the way his mother left her sentence unfinished he suspected other, less obvious calamities.

"Where is she?"

She inclined her head toward the small bedroom halfway down the corridor. Billy approached the closed door and knocked gently.

There was no response. He tried the doorknob, but it was locked.

"Cath-a-leen? Can I talk to you for a minute?"

There was no response.

There was another way of getting into the bedroom: the window which opened on the dining area where their mother slept. He leaned over a pile of shopping bags filled with old clothes at the foot of his mother's narrow cot and tugged on the window. It jammed easily unless you lifted it straight up on both sides at the same time, but this time it came right up.

Cathleen was stretched out on the twin bed which took up half the room's interior. Its pink quilt, made up neatly that morning before she left for work, was pulled across her legs. Her dark hair lay strewn across the fringed pillowcase. All he could see of her face was one side of her fine straight nose—their father's nose.

"Cath-a-leen?"

"Go away!" she replied. "Leave me alone!"

"Don't you wanna tell me what happened?"

"No. Leave me in peace. I don't want your help."

"That's a fine thing to say to your only brother. How do you think that makes me feel?"

"I don't care how it makes you feel," she said into the pillow.

He still could not see her entire face, but as best he could tell she had not suffered any injury, though it was clear she had been crying.

"Ma said you had an accident. Did you step in front of a truck?"

"No, I didn't step in front of a truck."

"A bicycle?"

"No. Just leave me alone."

"Something must have happened. Otherwise, you wouldn't be lying in there crying. Did you have some trouble with your boyfriend?"

He wasn't sure if she still had a boyfriend, but it seemed the most likely reason for a woman to cry.

"Jesus Christ," she said under her breath.

"Him too?"

She sprang up from the bed and made a lunge at the window. But it jammed as it always did unless you lowered it slowly. She pushed hard but was unable to budge it.

He watched in amazement, convinced something serious must have happened. She was not one to let her emotions get the best of her. Even when their father died, it was she who remained stoical throughout the wake and funeral, acting as a prop for their nearly demented mother. Cathleen was the pillar of the family, the one who inherited their father's dogged determination and steady temper.

"I think you'd better tell me what happened."

She fell back onto the bed again.

He gave the window a nudge and opened it wider. Then he leaned through, half in his mother's room, half in Cathleen's.

"Come on, Sis. Let's have it."

But she would tell him nothing. Exasperated, he returned to the living room where his mother was waiting in the narrow doorway, wringing her hands.

"She told you?"

"She didn't tell me nothing." He guided her back into the living room and sat her down on the old sofa. "Don't worry, Ma. It's gonna be okay."

But his mother's face was contorted into a grotesque expression he well remembered from his childhood when she seemed to cry so often, especially in the first months after his father's death. His inclination then was to cry along with her. But not today.

"I did all I could to raise her well. She's a good girl. Her father would be proud of her."

"Of course he would, Ma. Don't worry, nothing bad'll happen to her."

But she turned her reddened eyes on him as if in accusation and said, "Something already has!"

"What do you mean?"

It suddenly occurred to him that his sister had been sexually as-

92

saulted. That would explain her reluctance to talk as well as his mother's look of shame and anger. When they were kids it was usually Cathleen, the older child, who looked out for him and even fought his battles with neighborhood bullies. But this time it would be his turn to come to the rescue. He would kill the bastard. He would get the gun he had buried in the park and kill him.

He was so distracted by these thoughts, he didn't notice his mother had stopped crying.

"Billy, your sister's...pregnant. Oh, Jesus, Mary and Joseph!"

He was as shocked as if she had told him that she herself were with child, a woman in her mid-fifties who had had no truck with a man in more than a decade. Cathleen pregnant? Cathleen the Chaste? Cathleen the fucking mother superior?

He started to laugh.

"Billy! How can you?"

"Ma, you gotta be kidding. Who's the father, the Holy Ghost?"

"I won't have you talk about your sister that way! I won't have it!"

"I'm sorry, Ma. It's just so hard to imagine...Cath-a-leen... Well, you know..."

"It's no laughing matter."

"Okay, calm down. She can always get an abortion."

"What did you say?"

"I said she can get an abortion. How far gone can she be? One month? Two?"

But his mother looked as if he had spat at her.

"How could you even suggest such a thing? Do you realize what your father would say?"

"Ma, it's the tail-end of the twentieth century. Times have changed."

"Not in these matters. Why, if I had the strength I'd take you over to the sink and wash out your mouth with soap."

"Okay, Ma. Have it your way. Anyhow, I guess it's Cath-a-leen's decision. She's a grown woman, ain't she?"

"Sometimes I don't even recognize my own children. First that one comes home and tells me she's with child, and me not even knowing she had a steady boyfriend."

"You don't need to know somebody more than a couple minutes."

"Why, do you realize I didn't get pregnant with your sister until eight months after your father and I were married?"

"Some people are slow starters."

"I forbid you to talk any more about abortion in this house. Do you hear?"

"I hear, Ma, but that don't change nothing. What's she gonna do with the little brat? Leave it home for you to take care of?"

This thought apparently had not occurred to his mother. She digested its implications as quickly as she could.

"If necessary, I suppose she will."

"Sure. And you won't have any trouble taking care of a new baby, with your heart condition and all."

"I'll manage somehow. I raised the two of you, didn't I?"

"When you were twenty-five years younger. Get real, Ma. The best thing she could do is take a hike over to Planned Parenthood."

The words were scarcely out of his mouth before he felt her hand strike his cheek. It scarcely caused any pain, but she hadn't hit him like that since his early adolescence.

He reached for his jacket.

"Where are you going?"

"Gotta see a man about a horse."

"You're needed here. Don't you see that? Can't you think of someone besides yourself?"

"You seem to have the matter well in hand. Besides, you don't want me hanging around and infecting Cath-a-leen with my immoral ideas."

"This is no laughing matter, young man."

"Who's laughing? Do you see me laughing?"

"If you walk out of that door, don't come back," she said in the apocalyptic voice he remembered from his youth before she retreated into hypochondria. "I mean it. You contribute nothing to this family, morally or otherwise."

"Sure, Ma. Whatever you say."

He paused at the door, stung by her words but refusing to give her the satisfaction of showing it. Instead, he turned toward the long dark hallway and called, "See you later, Sis."

# CHAPTER TWELVE

The sting on his cheek reminded him of the way he used to feel when the other kids taunted him about his fatherless state. He was too young then to understand their need to belittle someone else the same way they themselves were constantly being put down by parents and teachers. He hadn't yet developed the ploy of acting crazy to scare such people off, but it was partly because of their taunting that he inadvertently did so. One day in the schoolyard some of his class-mates began chanting, "Billy Boy, Billy Boy, where's your daddy, Billy Boy?" He started swinging at every face he could reach, includ-ing the parish priest's who happened by and, seeing this one child beating up on all the others, assumed it was he who was the cause of the disturbance. Billy narrowly missed giving the man a broken nose but did succeed in bloodying it, an event which at the time seemed miraculous, since he had thought of priests as people who scarcely had any physical reality. He had never seen one urinate, much less bleed.

That lesson taught him how to handle future threats and insults. From that point on he was someone to be avoided, not taunted, and the epithet "Billy Boy" took on a new meaning.

As he made his way down 16th Street in pursuit of a handful of ups, the dark cloud in the back of his mind seemed about to over-whelm him, suffocate him with loneliness and worse. It was a mon-ster, a voracious beast which could only be appeased by offerings of powerful drugs dropped into its great maw. Today this dark god of his misery was demanding a major offering—a hefty dose of pharmaceu-tical-grade amphetamine.

He failed to recognize either of the tall Latinos loitering outside the bodega on the corner of 17th Street. He approached the older-looking one. The man regarded him cautiously out of the corner of one eye. Dealers and their lookouts were more in fear of someone like Billy who might be an undercover agent than he was of them.

"Come on, man. I need ups. I know I can get them here."

The man took a pull on his limp cigarette.

"What makes you think there's dope around here, man?"

"I can smell it," Billy said. "Look, I bought here before. I usually cop at the OTB, but I'm kind of hot at the moment."

"Whatchoo mean, 'hot'?"

"As in 'wanted.' By the police, man. I gotta lay low. That's why I gotta cop here."

The man laughed to himself—nerves, Billy sensed. He had been about this business long enough to read someone like this skinny Puerto Rican better than they could read him. He knew exactly what was going through the man's mind—rather, what wasn't going through it: the should-I and shouldn't-I that kept alternating as he waited for some sign to guide him like a mystic waiting for his god to speak. Sooner or later, Billy knew, he would get his pills. It was just a matter of being persistent. If people like this had to get a bona fides on every junkie who wanted to buy dope, they would never be able to stay in business.

Finally the man shrugged and jerked his head toward the corner.

"Talk to Ramon."

A few yards up from the intersection a shabbily dressed, shorter version of the Latino guarding the bodega was negotiating with a double-parked BMW. Billy hung back until the deal was over. Then, as the man turned toward him suspiciously, he said, "I'm looking to buy some ups."

The man only hesitated a couple seconds before making up his own mind about this particular customer. He glanced briefly toward the intersection, then as he walked toward the side entrance of the building said, "Follow me."

He felt the amphetamines even before he finished the Coke that washed them down. By the time he reached 9th Avenue he felt like he had just won the Irish Sweeps, or at least one of the school honor medals he had always coveted but never came close to winning. He greeted every familiar face along the four-block stretch of stores, along with some faces he didn't recognize. He hadn't had dope this good in months.

As he was approaching Scully's he spotted Andy Somers, yet another old schoolmate who was usually less than eager to run into him. But today Andy and the two other young men drinking beer out of quart containers on the sidewalk greeted him cheerfully.

"You're getting to be a regular celebrity, Billy. Charlie Madigan was looking for you. So was the C-POP."

"No shit?"

"Yeah," Andy said, clearly showing the effects of the container in his hand. "He says, 'You seen Billy Conover?' Of course, we says, 'Naw, we ain't seen him,' thinking maybe they wanted you for something other than to shake your hand, if you know what I mean."

Billy forced the corners of his mouth upward.

"So then Charlie says, 'You see him, try to find out where he's headed.' 'Sure, sure,' I says. 'You want him for something special?' Then he says, 'Yeah, something special.' So I figure, maybe you won the lottery or something, Billy, and they had the cops out looking to tell you the good news."

Andy winked and nudged his friend's ribcage.

"How long ago was this?" Billy asked.

"I dunno. How long ago would you say it was, guys? Half an hour? Three-quarters?"

"Thanks," Billy said, and started in the direction of Rosemary Grady's house.

He still had the illusion that he was thinking with superhuman clarity. He didn't hear the laughs of his two former classmates as they watched him walk away. Nor did it occur to him that Rosemary's would be one of the first places the police would be likely to look for him.

"Hide you out? Here? Are you out of your mind?"

"Put me in the cellar. Anyplace. You gotta help me, Rosy. They could send me up for ten years. I can't do no hard time, Rosy. They'd kill me in there."

"Billy, you know I'd do whatever I could for you. But I can't hide you here. It just won't work. Ain't there someplace else you could go?"

"No," he said, hanging his head over the kitchen table. "You got a newspaper?"

There was a day-old copy of the *Daily News* spread out on the floor where the baby had spit up.

"I gotta see today's paper. Right away."

"Maybe Mrs. Petrullo got one downstairs. I'll ask." He stared out the dirty kitchen windows at a gray tree in the yard. Cool it, he told himself. You don't know anything yet. Maybe what those two assholes told you was true, but maybe they were just pulling your leg. Maybe the newspaper will tell you something, maybe it won't. Don't panic yet.

"I got today's *Post*."

He skipped the headless torso on the cover and opened to page four. Sure enough, there was a small piece in a box on the lower right-hand side: BREAKTHROUGH IN BROOKLYN SLAYING....

"The Brooklyn District Attorney's office reported a major break-through in the case of the slaying of a black youth on Tuesday morning in Flatbush. Two youngsters playing in Prospect Park came upon the murder weapon which had apparently been buried there after the crime. A Parks Department ranger discovered the boys playing with the gun, a Colt 10 automatic, which they thought was a toy. The ranger brought the weapon to the police where Forensics identified it as the same gun used in the slaying of Andrew Mott, the youth worker killed early Tuesday morning in Flatbush...."

"Thanks," he said, already on his feet and heading toward the door.

"Where you off to now?"

"Don't know," he replied, halfway down the dark staircase. "I ain't been here, Rosy. I ain't been here at all."

When he reached the sidewalk he began walking toward 10th Avenue. When he reached Prospect Park he found the baseball diamonds occupied by small groups of boys intent on rushing the season. A few dogs and their owners were frolicking in the big common field shared by the diamonds. In the old days the fields had been surrounded by a chainlink fence. He and his friends used to play choose-up ball when no official game was in progress. He never played Little League—he was supposed to play on one of the parish teams but then got caught pissing into the common water bucket. After that, he had to content himself with kibitzing from the sidelines.

A softball came barreling across the greening grass and stopped almost at his feet. He bent down to pick up the ball as a young boy came running for it. On the infield were three more kids the same age.

"You guys need some coaching in a bad way."

He spent the next hour pitching and hitting pop flies and grounders. He was out of practice, but the kids didn't seem to notice. At first resentful of his intrusion, they soon accepted him and even chose up sides, with Billy acting as pitcher for both teams. Soon he forgot the reason he had come to the park.

"Thanks, mister," one of them said when it was time to leave. It was the first time he had ever been called "mister," and it made him feel old.

He watched them trek across the fields, the late-afternoon sun casting long shadows behind them. The diamonds were all empty now, with a different set of dogs exercising on the grass. Soon it would be dark. He hated the dark, even though he lived in it more than he did daylight. Darkness was the final end Sister told him was the fate of boys like himself who strayed from the path of grace. Darkness and hellfire. But hellfire had never seemed half as scary as the dark.

He reached into his pocket and popped the last of the amphetamines. Then he began walking north, keeping to the footpath at the edge of the field. It began to drizzle. Would the homeless woman return to her usual spot on the hill if it rained? If not, where did she go?

A couple ducks were waddling around the pond that fed off a small lake. The lake itself was overgrown with weeds, the old concrete landing where once you could rent paddle boats was fallen into disrepair and partially collapsed. Unconcerned with the deteriorating infrastructure, the ducks swam toward him in hopes of a handout.

"Sorry, chums."

The rain brought an early dusk. Soon he would be safe until morning came. But hiding out in the park wasn't the answer. He had to get out of town, out of the state, out of the country if possible.

He walked north again, keeping to the woods as much as possible. At Grand Army Plaza he headed for the subway. Once on a train he would be safe. What cop would single him out among the thousands of passengers on a subway train at rush hour?

But then he realized he had spent the last of his money on the drugs he had bought. Although he rarely paid to get into the subway, it would be foolhardy today to jump the turnstile. And he didn't dare panhandle the fare for fear of a cop spotting him.

"Boy, am I glad to see you."

The same pair of dark eyes that had comforted him the previous evening peered up suspiciously.

"Go away. I don't know you."

"What do you mean? It's Billy. I slept under that tree over there."

"Go away or I call the cops. Go away or I start screaming."

" Don't you remember? I got us coffee. I was a little...late bringing it."

Her eyes narrowed.

"You got coffee?"

"Right. I'm afraid I can't manage anything like that tonight on account of I'm flat broke. But I need a place to spend the night, and I was sort of hoping you would let me flop here again," he added in his most irresistible voice.

"I don't know no Billy. Get out of here. I'll scream for the cops. I mean it."

"Don't do that," he said, backing off. "See, I'm going."

# CHAPTER THIRTEEN

The pills were wearing off, and the panic they had temporarily muted began bubbling up to the surface of his consciousness. Before he did anything else, even before he decided what he must do to preserve his freedom, he had to get more ups. His addiction had a bizarre logic, but it was no less compelling than the logic by which other people lived. For those who needed cash to pay the rent, work made sense. For those like himself a chemical antidote against the evil inside his head was just as essential.

He would have to raise the cash by telephone, a medium which put him at a disadvantage, since he could be hung up on before bringing his full charms to bear.

"Where the hell you been? Everybody and his uncle's been calling for you."

"Does that include cops?"

"Why should the cops be looking for you?"

"You tell me, Brendan, me boy. The word's out that Charlie Madigan's all over the neighborhood. It's only logical he should stop by your place too."

"Charlie ain't been here. But your mother and Rosemary called. Even Cath-a-leen called."

"What for?"

"Said she was worried about you."

"Is that so? Well, I guess I just became very popular. Say, Bren, you sure the cops ain't been in touch? Maybe leaning on you a little about that friend of ours in Red Hook?"

There was just the slightest hesitation before Brendan's reply, but Billy's instinct told him it boded no good. He should hang up, it told him, tell Brendan he was calling from Manhattan or the Bronx. But the little boy inside him who so feared that dark void was screaming for help.

"Brendan, me bucko, I need you to do me a solid."

"What kind of solid, Billy? I'm a little short of cash at the moment."

"It's short cash that I want. A fiver'll do. Ten'll save me from perdition and guarantee a life of ease for at least the next twenty-four hours."

"Geez, I'd like to help you, Billy, but..."

"Them's the words I was waiting for, chum. This may seem a little strange, but I'd like you to bring the money over to the park."

"The park? It's dark out."

"That's very perceptive, Bren. But if you turn on the news tonight you'll find out why Charlie and his friends are looking for me. I swear to you, I had nothing to do with that yam's death. I was just going for a ride with Tommy McCready. Then Tommy stops the car and the guido riding shotgun gets out and wastes the yam. I couldn't believe it. I put as much distance as I could between that car and myself."

"Why didn't you tell me this before?"

"What difference would it make? This way you could say you know from nothing, and you wouldn't be lying."

"What about the gun, Billy?"

"What about the gun?"

"I mean, isn't that why the cops want you?"

"How did you know that, Brendan?"

There was another significant hesitation.

"You said the cops were looking for you, so I figure it must have something to do with the gun."

"I never mentioned no gun, Brendan."

"Sure you did. You said..."

"It sounds like maybe Charlie Madigan did pay you a visit."

"I swear to God, Billy."

"Maybe Charlie told you he was on to you about that fence over in the Hook. Maybe you even made a deal with Scumbag Charlie."

"On my mother's grave, Billy."

"Your mother ain't dead yet. Thanks for nothing."

If the police had been to Brendan's, it was reasonable to suppose they had also been to Rosemary's. But she wouldn't betray him. He dialed her number, glancing over both shoulders from the public phone at the corner of Third Street and Prospect Park West.

"If the cops are looking for you, Billy, you'd be crazy to come here."

"You got a point there, Rosy. On the other hand, it gets a little damp in Prospect Park at night this time of year."

"You got no place to go?"

"That's about the size of it. Actually, I was hoping you could loan me a couple dollars and then I could make other arrangements."

"How'm I gonna do that, Billy? You know my check don't come until first of the month."

"I was hoping you might have a few bucks salted away for emergencies."

"I ain't got a red cent, Billy, and that's the goddamn truth."

"No way you could lay your hands on something for me? I mean, as a special favor?"

"How'm I gonna do that? Everybody I know is either waiting for her check or is so pissed at me they wouldn't give me the time of day, never mind five dollars."

"I was thinking more in the line of...a customer."

"Customer?"

There was a pause, then a sniffling sound on the other end of the line.

"Rosy, you still there?"

"I never thought I'd hear them words out of your mouth, Billy. Not after all I done for you."

"I'm sorry Rosy, I really am. It's just that I really need the money. It's kind of like a matter of life or death. My death."

More sniffling. Then, " Somebody wants to kill you?"

"Well, they want to put me away for fifteen or twenty years with a bunch of maniacs and child molesters. Same thing."

"Jesus, Billy," she said, still in need of a tissue. "I wish I could do something to help. But you don't know how bad it hurts when you say something like that."

"Say what, Rosy? It's no secret you pick up a few dollars here and there. Everybody in the neighborhood knows that."

"Oh, Billy!"

"What'd I say? I ain't passing no judgment on you. Jesus, Rosy, you ain't gonna play Queen of the May with me, are you?"

"I always wanted to be Queen of the May, Billy. I bet you don't believe that. But every year I prayed Sister would pick me. But she always picked Doris Grumbach or Mary Ann Powers. I just wanted to walk at the front of that procession once, right behind Our Lady's statue. That's all I wanted."

"I'm sorry about that, Rosy. I really am. If I could make you Queen of the May, I would. I really would. Only, my influence with the powers that be is kind of weak these days, if you know what I mean."

"Now you're making fun of me!"

"I'm not. Really, I'm not. It's just I've got these other things on my mind, like going to jail with a bunch of black faggots who pump iron all day and wait for some white boys to turn up so's they can butt-fuck their brains out. I'm really sorry you never got to be Queen of the May, Rosy. Only, I can think of better ways to die than getting AIDS from some two-ton gorilla who's already stabbed his mother to death and eaten her for breakfast. I'm sorry, Rosy. I guess I should be thinking more about my fellow man."

"You're such a fucking wise-ass, Billy Conover," she said, her sinuses abruptly cleared. "You don't give two shits about me, and you never did. All I am is a goddamn hole. You want a blowjob, call Rosy O'Grady. You need some bread, call Rosy. I'm getting sick of it, Billy. I'm fed up, if you want to know the truth."

"Rosy, what the fuck are we arguing about? All I'm asking you for is five lousy bucks. If I had some other way of getting it, do you think I'd be bothering you?"

"No, that's right, you wouldn't. In fact, I wouldn't even hear from you until you got horny again. Then it would be Rosy Honey, and Rosy Sweetie. Jesus, Billy, you're as easy to see through as a pane of glass."

"I'm sorry you think that way, Rosy. You don't understand the real feelings I have for you."

"That's right, I don't," she said, lapsing into tears again. "Because I don't believe you *have* any real feelings for me. Nobody does. All they want's one thing, and after they get it they're gone so fast they hardly have time to zip their zippers."

"Rosy, just five bucks. For me, Billy Boy. I'll never ask you anything like this again, I swear."

"What d'you care what people say about me? What d'you care if they call me the Whore of 16th Street?"

"Please, Rosy. Just this once."

There was silence on the other end of the line. But the tears had stopped.

"I'll lay low for a couple hours, then I'll come by your place. I know you won't let me down. I know I can count on you."

He waited an hour before venturing out of the park again. By now he was chilled through. Again, he took the long way around, exiting well below 10th Avenue this time in case someone was laying for him. But there was no way he could conceal his final approach to Rosy's house.

Scully's neon was shining red and blue. The streetlight at the corner of 16th Street was the same green as the crossing light on the electric trains his father had set up for him the Christmas before he died. It seemed impossible that this world, the little neighborhood he had lived in for the past two decades, could come to an end just because of one stupid mistake he had made. It made no more sense than if someone were to tell him that a minute from now a meteor would fall out of the sky and end his life. No more illicit adventures with Brendan. No more arguments with Cathleen about who left hair in the bathtub drain. It was too much to believe. It was like his father's death, which he still dreamed was not true and had all been a mistake, there his old man was, washing up for dinner just as he used to. Why did he still dream that dream after all these years? Why couldn't he accept that his father would never come home again or toss a ball with him in Prospect Park, or take him and his sister and mother out for a ride in the country?

The cold wind whipping down 16th Street yanked him back to reality. The fact is, Billy Boy, it told him, you stepped in it bad this time. All you can do is try to get your ass out of this city and start a new life someplace else. Anyplace else. With any luck, the guido who actually pulled the trigger will fess up, or somebody will rat on him, and the rest of the jerks in the car that night will become history, not worth scouring an entire country for.

He'd always had a notion to see the Rocky Mountains. This was as good a time as any to make good on that ambition.

Rosy's stoop was deserted. The rain had driven the sidewalk drinkers inside Scully's. In a minute or two an "F" train would pull into the station under his feet and disgorge a few dozen commuters. He hurried up the stoop and pushed hard on Rosy's bell. A moment later the buzzer sounded and he stepped into the dark vestibule.

"Who is it?" Rosy called.

"It's me."

The hallway was warm and welcoming after the long soaking-through he had had. He took off his denim jacket as he started up the dim staircase toward the shaft of light showing from Rosy's kitchen. He felt his shirt and found that it too was wet. He was hoping Rosy had a spare shirt on the premises when the door at the top of the stairs opened wide and someone much taller and muscular than Rosemary Grady stepped out on the landing.

Billy paused, then started taking backsteps down the staircase. The figure at the top of the stairs said nothing.

"Rosy?"

"Hold it right there!" a voice called behind him.

He turned and saw a young cop crouched in firing position.

"Just keep stepping back down the steps like you was doing, Billy," the figure at the top of the stairs told him. "When you get to the bottom, put your hands up against the wall and spread your legs. You don't pull nothing funny, Billy, nobody gets hurt."

"Is that you Charlie?" Billy said, still not moving. "Jesus, Charlie, you gave me a scare. Is Rosy okay? I was just coming by to see if she was okay. I was talking to her on the phone a little while ago and she says there was a prowler in the building."

"Just do as I say, Billy, and we don't have no problem."

"Charlie, you don't think the prowler was me, do you? It's Billy Conover. You remember, the kid who used to tease you in the schoolyard."

As soon as the words were out of his mouth, he regretted them. It was the first time he could remember his wits deserting him like that.

"I mean, not that you didn't do your own share of teasing too, Charlie."

"Billy, I'm gonna tell you for the last time. Back down the stairs and put your hands against the wall or you're gonna regret it."

He could tell that Charlie meant it. This was a moment he  must have looked forward to, a get-even he had waited fifteen years for.

He slowly back-stepped to the landing at the bottom of the stairs. As soon as his foot hit the last creaky step he felt his body slam into the wall as if of its own accord. His arms were yanked painfully behind his back and the icy jaws of handcuffs bit into his wrists.

He was back in the same dull green room he had been in the day before. The same detective was interrogating him.

This time there was no hot coffee or cigarettes. The big cop didn't even bother to greet him. He just walked into the room, dropped a file on the table and sat down heavily. Then he lit a cigarette, the smoke of which turned Billy's empty stomach, and stared at the wall next to the table as if trying to recall what he had had last night for supper. Finally he glanced at the young man seated across from him as if he had never before laid eyes on him.

"Okay, Billy, let's go over it again."

He opened the folder. Billy tried to make out what was written in it, but the cop's scrawl was miniscule and impossible to read upside down. The folder reminded him of a doctor's or dentist's, although no doctor's record would have contained the rap sheet he saw poking out from beneath the sheets of handwritten notes. He knew what was on that arrest record—two possessions, and a time-served for the trash can he threw through that plate-glass window. The possessions never even went to court.

"Tuesday night you go over to Roche's Funeral Parlor where you get into a fist fight with one of the mourners. The wake breaks up at about nine o'clock, and then you go...where was it?"

"First I went home, then I went to my friend Brendan's."

"Where does Brendan live?"

Billy told him.

"And you stay there until...what was it you said—one in the morning?"

Despite his aching wrists and belly, Billy smiled at the cop's transparent subterfuge.

"Actually, I stayed there for the rest of the night, Lieutenant. Brendan can vouch for that."

"Sergeant, Billy. Just plain sergeant. Suppose I told you, Billy, your friend Brendan wasn't sure whether or not you went out for a while Monday night. Suppose he just couldn't recall one way or the other. Is there anyone else who could vouch for your whereabouts, say, between midnight and 3:00 a.m.?"

Billy pretended to think hard about this. Then he said, "Brendan has a cat, but she sleeps most of the time and anyways a jury probably wouldn't consider her testimony reliable."

The cop regarded him as if he wanted to slap the teeth out of his mouth.

"We're not here to play games, Billy. You answer my questions directly. You understand that?"

"Yes...Sergeant," Billy replied, almost saying, "Brother."

"Suppose we go over it again."

This time they started with where Billy had dinner that night and even what he ate, and then traced his whereabouts for the rest of his evening, hour by hour. It was hard for him to understand the point of this kind of questioning. His story was simple enough. There was little chance of the cop's catching him in an inconsistency. Everything hinged on Brendan's vouching for him. And if Brendan had already let him down, what was the point to going over the same lie again and again? Why not just book him? But if Brendan was standing firm, did this big dumb flatfoot think he, Billy, was suddenly going to confess to being party to a murder?

Half an hour later, they were no further along. The cop had smoked three cigarettes. Billy had smoked two, although he rarely smoked and didn't enjoy it. Finally, the cop parked half of his big rear end on the table, picked a piece of tobacco out of his front teeth and said, "You know, Billy, you give us the shooter, we can make you a deal. Maybe even get you off with probation."

He couldn't help but give this offer some thought. He had little care for whether he added anything to his rap sheet, not even if it was a serious offense like accessory to a murder, so long as he didn't go to jail. On the other hand, he was not about to be suckered into something the cop could never pin on him anyway, never mind what Bruno's friends might do to him if he ratted.

"And if I really don't know nothing about it like I said?"

The detective took a drag on what was left of his cigarette. Billy noted his tobacco-stained fingers, the same stains he used to see on his father's own.

"In that case you have to look out for yourself. If we get the trigger man and he says you was with him, you swing too. If he says you weren't, you walk. Only you yourself know where you really were."

"I already told you that."

"You told me what you thought would save your neck. But you better think some more. Suppose, for instance, we already have some of the people who was in the car that night? Suppose we have the driver, say. And suppose the only thing that's keeping a felony murder charge from landing him in the slammer for the next fifteen years is a deal he cuts to name everyone else in the car? Not just the perp, but all of you. You think friendship's gonna keep him from fingering you? You think he's gonna do fifteen-to-twenty when all he has to say is Billy Conover was in the back seat? Not doing nothing. Just minding his own business, maybe. He ain't saying you pulled no trigger or egged nobody on. You was just sitting there minding your business. But if saying that gets him five years instead of fifteen, you think he ain't gonna spill his guts?"

"You make it sound like it's already a done deal."

The cop shrugged and slid off the tabletop.

"I just want you to have something to think about, Billy. You could walk out of here and think you made monkeys of us. But if we got somebody who can finger you and does, your ass is history. So what you got here is what you might call a window of opportunity. You tell us who the guido was that pulled the trigger and we put in a good word for you at the D.A.'s."

"You already know it was a wop?"

The cop pretended to look surprised.

"Did I say 'guido'? That must have been a slip of the tongue. I must have had Bensonhurst on my mind."

"Sure. Does that mean I can leave now?"

"Who said anything about leaving? We still got more questions to ask. That is, after you decide whether or not you're gonna cooperate—which I sincerely think you will."

The detective nodded toward the doorway where a uniformed officer had been waiting. The cop put the cuffs back on Billy and led him away.

He had found rat hairs in his food at the Brooklyn House of Detention during his stay there a couple years earlier, and had to constantly look over his shoulder when he wasn't locked up in his cell. But the conditions in the House of D had it all over the holding cells of the 72nd Precinct.

There was no running water and just one toilet for five prisoners. He knew legally they couldn't hold him here for very long and that the real reason for his being locked up was to wear him down psychologically. But knowing this didn't make the place smell any better. He asked about getting a lawyer and was told they would contact legal aid for him. But then he decided that asking for a lawyer might make it look as if he actually was guilty of something. So he decided to wait them out, at least for the night, even though he would get very little sleep on the concrete floor and had to keep one eye open on his cellmates.

Two were Latino, the other three black. Each group kept to themselves, making him odd man out. He tried to start up conversations, but the Latinos barely spoke English and the blacks acted as if they suspected him of being a spy.

Sometime past midnight he dozed off. He was awakened soon after by a young cop dragging his nightstick across the bars. He had a bunch of paper bags in his arms.

"Supper time," he said and dropped the bags onto a moist patch of concrete just inside the cell. Everyone made a scramble for the food. After they had eaten, a calm descended. Shortly afterward the same cop who had brought the sandwiches called Billy forward, cuffed him and led him back upstairs to the interrogation room.

"Bad news, Billy. Your buddy McCready's given you up."

"Is that so?"

"This may be your last chance to tell us what we need to know."

The cop was grinning as if he really did have the case broken. But there was no way of Billy's knowing for sure.

"Of course, it don't matter all that much now whether you chime in or not. We have enough evidence to get a conviction on the shooter without you. All I'm saying is, you still got a chance to save your neck if you want. If not, well, I guess you know what it's like being locked up with them low-lifes."

Billy was trying to think fast, but the lack of sleep and the ham sandwich he had just eaten made that process difficult. He could have used a cup of coffee, but no one was offering any.

"Think it over, Billy. But don't take too long. The bus leaves for the House of D in five hours."

He remembered how he had felt when he found those rat hairs in his potato salad. Even returning to the damp cell in the precinct basement and spending another five hours on the cold concrete seemed more than he could endure.

"I don't need to think no more about it. I'll tell you what you want to know."

# CHAPTER FOURTEEN

He had decided he would only give up the goon who actually pulled the trigger. He didn't remember anybody else's name anyway, with the exception of Tommy McCready, and the cops already knew Tommy was the driver.

But it wasn't that easy. The detective who reminded him so much of his mother's brothers didn't believe him.

"You just get into a car and take a ride to nowhere for the fun of it? You didn't know they were going to Flatbush? You didn't know there was baseball bats and chains on the floor of the backseat? And you didn't know the guido up front was packing an automatic?"

"You gotta remember, they were giving out free dope. By the time we reached Ocean Parkway I didn't care if they were going to the moon. I didn't know what they were up to until Tommy pulls over to the curb and everybody gets out. I never saw no gun until it was too late."

"You didn't know the guido had a piece."

"Right. Look, I might do something stupid now and then, Sergeant, but I'm not totally brainless. Why would I want to get mixed up in a killing? It ain't my style. Any of the beat cops in this precinct can tell you that."

The detective took time out to glance at Billy's folder again.

"Let's see. Possession. Malicious Mischief."

"The Possessions was dismissed for insufficient evidence. I got time-served for the Mischief."

"You managed to stay pretty clear of jail, considering the life of crime you've led."

"What life of crime? I've just had trouble finding a job, what with this here recession. Look, I don't wanna be a pest or nothing, but how soon can I get out of this place? I've told you all I know."

"Relax, Billy. You're doing fine."

The cop looked through some loose sheets of paper lying next to Billy's folder. He picked up the top sheet and began reading to himself. As he did so, he began pacing—a few steps one way, then a slow turn and a couple paces back. Billy noted a button had come off the lower end of his white shirt, exposing his hairy stomach. His suit needed a cleaning.

The detective put the paper down and placed both hands on the table.

"Let's go over it again: McCready's car pulls up. He asks if you want to go for a ride. No place special. Just a ride. You don't recognize none of the other people in the car. How many did you say there were? Five?"

"Four."

"Okay, four other people in the car. And you say you didn't know none of them but Tommy, right?"

"Right."

"But you get in the car anyway. Just for the hell of it. To take a little spin around the block. Whatever. Then what happens?"

"Somebody offers me a couple pills."

"Any pills in particular?"

The big cop was hanging directly over him. Billy could smell the deodorant he used, mixed with day-old sweat.

"No."

"This generous person, he was in the backseat or the front?"

"The back, I think. I don't remember. Yeah, the back."

The detective hesitated, his face red from the exertion of supporting his large frame on the tabletop. Billy wondered if his complexion might also be the result of a drinking problem. He hoped not. Cops who drank were bad news.

"Okay. So what happens next?"

"I took them."

"You swallowed them?"

"Right."

"With what?"

"Nothing."

"No water? Beer? Nothing?"

"Beer."

"Okay, then what?"

"We keep riding."

"Down past the park. Then on Ocean Parkway."

"Correct."

"When did you turn off the parkway?"

"I don't remember. I was starting to feel the ups by then."

"Did anybody say anything about where they were headed?"

"No."

"You're sure?"

"If they did I wasn't paying no attention. Like I said, I was digging my high."

The cop stood up straight.

"Nobody said nothing about wasting some yams?"

"Not that I remember."

"It wouldn't have been memorable if they did?"

"Yeah, it would. I just don't remember nothing like that. Hey," Billy said, sitting up straight despite his fatigue, "if I had the foggiest notion they was gonna commit a murder I would've been out of there."

"How about if they were just gonna crack a few skulls? You out then too?"

"Sure," Billy said.

"And you never saw no baseball bats."

"Right."

"Even though they were probably right on the floor beneath your feet."

"You got it. Like I said, I was into my high."

The cop turned a chair around and sat down on it, his big shoulders straining against the cheap fabric of his suit.

"You get high pretty often, don't you Billy."

"Not all that often."

"Four, five times a week?"

"Less than that."

"Tell me, Billy, where do you get the bread? You already told me you ain't working."

"I get money from home."

"You steal it?"

"My mother gives a me a couple bucks, you know, for travel expenses."

"So you can look for a job."

"Right."

"But you spend it on dope."

"Sometimes. It don't cost all that much. All I take is a couple pills. Pharmaceutical amphetamine."

"You got a prescription?"

Billy checked to see if the cop was making a joke, but his face was deadpan.

"No, I ain't got no prescription."

"So, how do you get it?"

"I ask a friend."

"What kind of friend?"

"You know, somebody who can help me out. Look," he said, his fatigue and hunger getting the best of him, "I don't hurt nobody. I feel bad sometimes, really bad, you know? Like, about myself and everything. So I take a couple pills. They make me feel better for a while."

"But you wouldn't call yourself a junkie."

"No, I wouldn't."

"And you wouldn't, say, commit a crime to help support your habit, like maybe climbing in somebody's window and helping yourself to their jewelry."

"Who told you that?"

"Told me what? That you're a junkie or that you do petty burglaries?"

Billy didn't want to choose, so he said nothing.

The cop turned the chair around and sat on it in normal fashion. Suddenly he didn't look tired or overweight.

"Billy, I'm gonna level with you. We could put your ass in a big sling. We could tie you to half a dozen burglaries just over the past three months."

"No way."

"You could do serious time. No more dismissals because the judge feels sorry for you or because he thinks you're too white and pretty to send upstate with the spics and niggers. The only one can save you is yourself. You got no friends no more. You understand what I'm saying? The only one you can count on is yourself. So, if there's anything

115

else you can tell us about what happened that night, you better do it while there's still time. Once this goes to the judge, your fate is in his hands and it'll be too late to make any deals."

Billy lowered his eyes. Suddenly he felt like crying like he hadn't done since he was a little kid. He said, "I already told you all I know. I just went along for the ride. I had no idea they was gonna do nothing like what they done."

"And when it all started to go down, you just ran away, right?"

"No, I didn't."

"You stood and watched. Then you drove away with them."

"I never shot nobody. I didn't even hit nobody with a bat."

"It don't matter, Billy," the cop said, leaning across the desk. Billy was appalled by the strength of the urge he felt to throw his arms around this big cop and cry his eyes out. Instead, he sat up straighter to try to put more distance between them.

"Billy, don't you see what I'm tryna tell you? You were there. You were with them. You got in the car, you rode with them, and you stood with them while they wasted the yam. Then you got back in the car again and drove away. You were an accessory, Billy."

The cop stood up and lit a cigarette.

"Alright, so I was with them. I already admitted that. What else can I tell you? Nothing."

"Yes, you can, Billy. You know we've got the gun. And your prints are on it. Now, make up your mind. Are you gonna swing for that murder, or are you gonna give us the punk that actually pulled the trigger? It's your decision."

It had never once occurred to Billy that he could be tried for the murder, even if the police found out it was he who had buried the gun. He still didn't even know why the killing took place. People did crazy things. He did crazy things himself, although he drew the line when it came to serious violence. He had assumed the black kid was a drug dealer or somebody who had cheated his killer out of something. That was what most murders were about. There was no law to protect drug dealers from each other's dishonesties, so they had to act as their own law-enforcement.

The detective asked Billy to sign a written statement.

He spent the rest of the night dozing against cold iron bars. He was awakened in the usual fashion and given breakfast, a bag containing tepid coffee and a doughnut. Then nothing happened for the better part of an hour until he and his cellmates were cuffed and led out of the cell and into a van parked at the side of the precinct. From there they were driven downtown to the House of Detention near the big department stores where his mother used to take him for new blue pants and shirts at the start of each new school year.

To his surprise, Tommy McCready was arraigned at the same time as himself. Only, Tommy had a private lawyer, while Billy had to make do with a Legal Aid attorney. He'd had dealings with Legal Aid following his previous arrests and didn't think much of them. But this one was a young, attractive woman.

She scarcely glanced his way before opening his file and saying, "You cop to Reckless Endangerment and I get you eighteen months on the Rock."

"Eighteen months?" he said, her charms rapidly dissipating at the prospect of spending the next year and a half on Riker's Island. "The sergeant promised me a deal if I cooperated."

"This *is* the deal, Mr. Conover. If you didn't cooperate you'd be facing an accessory charge, minimum. You testify for the prosecution, and with good behavior you'll be out of jail in a year's time. You don't, and you can be looking at ten-to-fifteen upstate."

They were seated at a big wooden table inside the bar but out of earshot of the other people in the courtroom. Billy glanced at Tommy, but Tommy was absorbed in conversation with his own lawyer, a nattily dressed man with an expensive weave job. It was hard to see how any judge or jury would take the word of a sharpy like that over the lovely creature defending his own case.

"What do I have to say?"

"Everything you know about what happened that night."

"And who watches my ass, you should excuse my French, when I get off the Rock?"

"Mr. Conover, I'm authorized to make you the deal I just offered. If you choose to turn it down, that's your business. But my advice is a year at Riker's beats any kind of time in a real lockup. What happens when you get out of prison is something you can think about in the meantime."

"Okay," he said, feeling there was no way he was going to be able to appeal to anything but the hardened lawyer inside this shell of a female. "Let's get it over with."

"First things first. First, you enter a plea of guilty to Reckless Endangerment. Then we try to get you out of here on a reasonable bail."

"How'm I gonna raise bail?"

He glanced around the all-but-empty courtroom. There were three women sitting a couple rows back from the bar, one of whom he recognized as Tommy's sister.

"We'll try to make it bond. Is anyone in your family employed?"

"My sister."

"Is she willing to guarantee bond for you?"

"You have to ask her."

"No, *you'll* have to ask her, Mr. Conover," the lawyer said, making him wish she wouldn't keep calling him by his last name: It made it sound as if she were talking about someone else. "After arraignment they'll let you make one phone call. I suggest that it be to your sister. I'll do what I can in the meantime to make sure bail is reasonable."

# CHAPTER FIFTEEN

"You certainly stepped in it this time," Cathleen told him as they rode home together on the #75 bus. "You damn near gave Mom a heart attack. One of these days you'll finish her off."

He was gazing out the window, marveling at how wonderful everything looked from the vantage of freedom. Even his sister seemed to have a radiance about her. She was wearing a blue business suit, her makeup freshly applied, good-looking enough to land a role in a movie.

"And I don't appreciate having to take time off my job to bail my jailbird brother out. I had to lie to my boss that I had a stomach ache."

"Pretty soon that'll be true," Billy said, absorbed in the passing landscape of dry cleaners and small Italian groceries. He didn't notice the dirty look his sister gave him, nor take note of the silence that followed until they had made the turn off Court Street and he saw a lonely tear trickling down her cheek. "Hey, I didn't mean nothing, Sis. You know I'm grateful."

"Just see you get your ass into court when you're supposed to, so I don't have my salary garnisheed."

"You bet I will," he said, making a move to take her hand but thinking better of it. "You can count on it."

His mother treated him as if he had just returned from the wars and insisted on making breakfast, eggs and bacon which the family usually only had on Sundays. His sister left them to each other, making no pretense of hiding her disgust.

"Won't you have something to eat before you go, dear?"

"If I take one more breath of fried bacon I'll barf."

That was as close as she had come to talking about her pregnancy, which her mother now accepted as merely another fact of life like the change of the seasons. She had even begun to knit booties for the new arrival. It was a reaction several other mothers on the block had already experienced. The only difference was that those other daughters had no careers or any particular ambition but illegitimate motherhood to look forward to.

"Would you like a piece of crumb cake, Billy?" she said, getting up to look for the Entenmanns that had been on top of the refrigerator for the past week.

"Thanks, Ma, I'm full."

"Coffee?"

"Don't mind if I do."

She turned to draw more water into the kettle from the old trough-style kitchen sink that reminded Billy of communal urinals he used to see in retreat houses. The water made a racket as it hit the kettle's empty bottom. She filled it nearly full even though she was only going to boil enough for one cup. Then she set it down on the grease-covered stove and lit a match to the jet beneath it.

"What are your plans for today, Billy?" she asked as if he had just been demobilized from the Infantry.

"I thought I might catch a few winks. Then I figure I go job hunting."

The job-hunting idea was not just the usual line he fed her to cover up a variety of activities ranging from movie watching to shoplifting booze in local supermarkets. He knew his chances of getting probation for the crime he had admitted to were greatly enhanced if he turned up for his next court appearance with gainful employment. There was nothing judges, lawyers and other respectable people liked better than that someone should tie the same ball and chain to their leg that they themselves were tied to.

He fell asleep without difficulty on the living room sofa. But he was troubled by bad dreams about Tommy's friends coming after him. In one dream the murderer confronted him with a pistol whose barrel was more than a foot long. Instead of firing it, he tried to shove it down Billy's throat.

He awoke gagging on the taste of greasy bacon and barely made it to the bathroom before throwing up.

He cleaned up, shaved and told his mother he was going out to look for a job. As he was heading toward the door, she put a crumbled bill in his hand. He thought at first it was just a five but then saw the two and zero on it.

"Ma, I don't need all this."

"It's good to have a couple extra dollars, just in case," she said, the smell of her dusting powder strong as any perfume. He winced, knowing what he would really use the money for, but realized he didn't have the character or will or whatever strength it was that would allow him to act otherwise.

He headed for Rosemary Grady's house. He knew Rosemary sometimes had a stash on the premises, but even more important at the moment, she would be willing and able to relieve the sexual energies that had been building up in him.

He found the outside door of her building locked. He pushed the top bell, and a moment later Rosemary's head appeared in the second-story window.

"What's with the locked door?"

"My landlady doesn't want no more visitors except family."

"Well, I'm family. Let me in."

"I'm sorry, Billy," she said, looking as if she had just washed her hair and was getting ready to dry it. That meant she didn't have any clothes on under her bathrobe.

"Just for a minute, Rosy. I just got sprung from the slammer and I was thinking about you the whole time I was there."

"I'm really sorry, Billy, but I can't afford to get evicted."

He glanced toward the parlor-floor windows. A nod from Rosemary confirmed his suspicions.

She said, "I'm sorry, Billy, I really am," only this time she jerked her head toward the back of the house where a fire escape gave access both to the roof and to her apartment below. There was an empty lot just two houses away. The fence surrounding it was eight feet high, but he had climbed higher fences.

Even so, he would have to wait for nightfall. He resigned himself to an afternoon of celibacy and turned his attention to figuring out where he could lay his hands on some ups. Brendan was the likeliest option. Besides, he had a few questions to ask his friend about how the police came by their knowledge about a certain fence in Red Hook. Brendan wasn't home. From the looks of his apartment—a two-day-old doughnut on the rug being feasted on by several cockroaches; the shades drawn on the sunny day outside—he had apparently not spent the night there either.

He searched the apartment but found no drugs. Then the telephone rang.

"McCauley residence."

He heard breathing at the other end of the line—not the heavy breathing of a pervert but the hesitant pants of someone whose nerves were on edge.

"One more chance. Speak now or forever hold your peace or whatever it is you happen to be holding."

He thought no more about the call until he was out on the street again. Then it occurred to him it might not have been intended for Brendan but for himself. In his experience, cops were not given to heavy breathing under such circumstances. Could it have been one of the thugs who were in the car the night the black kid was wasted? Did someone find out he had been talking to Detective Sergeant McCaffrey?

Dr. Griswald's office was nearly deserted at this time of day—just one old woman and a nondescript gent who might have drifted in for an afternoon nap. Billy marched up to the receptionist, a heavy middle-age woman with patent-leather hair who looked as if she might be just as content taking numbers, and told her he had to see the doctor on an emergency basis.

"And what is the emergency?" she asked between chews of a thick wad of gum.

"I have an acute pain in my right side," he said, clutching his ribcage. "I think I have appendicitis."

The woman glanced at his midsection—he had inadvertently grabbed his left rather than his right side—and raised her heavily penciled eyebrows.

"I'm sorry, Mr. Conover, but the doctor is full up this morning. You'll have to come back later."

"But what about my appendicitis?"

She smiled out of one side of her mouth and resumed filling out some Medicaid forms, most of which, Billy knew, would be submitted in triplicate. "I suggest you try the Methodist Hospital emergency room."

He glanced again at the other two patients. The old lady was talking to an invisible companion. The man had dozed off.

"The doctor has a patient in there right now?"

"The doctor is in consultation on the telephone."

He walked past the receptionist's desk and into the inner sanctum. Both examining rooms were empty. He headed for the office at the back end of the building. The door was closed, but he only paused long enough to knock once before entering.

"Yes, of course," the startled physician said into an old black telephone as Billy let himself in. "Can I call you back? Go ahead with that business we were discussing. I'll make sure it comes out right for you."

"A little professional transaction?" Billy said.

The doctor grinned painfully. Billy used to be a regular customer, although Griswald probably preferred to call him a patient. That was four or five years ago when Billy's drug use included a cornucopia of controlled substances. Nor was Billy the doctor's only such "patient." In fact, it had been the proliferation of young men and women like himself that eventually put a stop to the doctor's prolific prescription writing. But the state only suspended his license for six months.

"I do generally require an appointment, Billy," Griswald said, his thin gray hair combed meticulously. He wore suits that seemed to wear him, brown and other off-color affairs which his wife, or somebody, seemed to buy off the rack in thrift shops.

"But in my case you'll make an exception."

"What can I do for you?"

"I need a 'scrip."

"A prescription?"

"Excuse me, yes, a prescription."

"For...?"

"Amphetamines."

The doctor began to rocked gently as if he were in complete control of the situation, although from the nervous tremor of his thin lips it was clear he was not.

"You know, Billy, I can't just write a prescription on demand."

"Since when?"

The doctor tried to smile again, but it turned into a grimace. He was a short man whose head barely reached the back of his big swivel chair and whose feet, Billy suspected, did not extend to the worn rug under his feet.

"Prescriptions are only for the use of patients with real medical problems."

"Oh, I got me a medical problem, okay."

"Yes? What is it?"

"Clinical depression."

The doctor cocked his head to one side and tried to look amiable.

"That sounds like something for a psychiatrist to deal with. I only treat physical ailments."

"It's a physical ailment, okay."

"It is?"

"Sure. Because when I can't get any ups I get physically violent. Sometimes I bust up the first thing I see. Like this office here."

"I see."

"I've even been known to bust a doctor in the nose now and then. I get pretty fucking uncontrollable."

The doctor reached for his prescription pad.

"Under the circumstances..." he said, searching for his pen. Billy spotted it under some papers and handed it to him.

After he had finished writing, Griswald took a deep breath and said, "I'm warning you, Billy: Don't tell anyone about this. I'm only doing this on an emergency basis. If you want to see me in the future, you'll have to make an appointment just like any other patient."

"Sure, sure."

"By rights I should send you to Doctor Feinstein. But I happen to know he's on vacation. That's the only reason I'm prescribing a few of these. They're low-dose and are only to be taken as indicated."

"Right," Billy said, noting the good doctor was in fact writing a prescription for ten high-voltage whammies. He watched the man sign his name with a ridiculous flourish that he himself had forged more than once.

"You forgot to check the generic box."

"Yes. Of course," the doctor said, correcting his oversight.

Billy snatched the slip of paper out of his hand.

"Thanks, Doc. Don't forget to send me a bill."

# CHAPTER SIXTEEN

He returned to his mother's house to wait for nightfall. But his mother's mood had changed radically from what it had been earlier in the day. She seemed preoccupied and only acknowledged his presence long enough to tell him not to step on the wet kitchen floor.

As he left the house in search of more congenial company, he noticed a green Bonneville parked across the street, its windows heavily tinted. He started to walk toward 9th Avenue, then turned to see if the car was still there. It was just pulling away from the curb. By the time he reached 9th Avenue it had almost pulled even with him.

He walked rapidly across the intersection. The car kept pace with him. When he reached the vacant lot near Rosemary's house, he abruptly came to a halt. The car stopped too. He turned and doubled back to the subway entrance. The car waited until he had started down the subway stairs, then slowly pulled away.

Brendan's mother lived in a two-family house in Bay Ridge. She owned the house, as she did the building in which her son lived, along with a couple other properties in Canarsie. How she came by her money—Brendan's father had deserted the family when Brendan was barely old enough to remember him—was a mystery. Billy had never thought of her as anything but a sweet if slightly goofy old doll. But during the ride on the slow-moving "R" train he found himself wondering about the source of her wealth. An insurance policy she collected on when the elder McCauley died? A bonanza the man bequeathed to her in a fit of conscience over his earlier desertion, money won at the gaming tables of Las Vegas or dealing pork bellies on the stock market? Or had some other relative left her a wad of cash which that seemingly simpleminded woman then parlayed into a small fiefdom?

But why was it that her son scarcely owned a television that worked and had to resort to robbing neighbors to supplement the small income he earned collecting her rents?

"Hello, Mrs. McCauley," he said to the small pink woman who opened the door for him. She peered up at him through watery brown eyes, her mouth half-open. "It's Billy, Mrs. M. Billy Conover."

She stared at him like a troll contemplating a giant. Then someone seemed to pull a string attached to her brain and she suddenly came to life.

"You've grown so much!"

She said the same thing every time he made one of these semi-annual visits to track down Brendan. He hadn't grown an inch in four years.

"Brendan here?" he asked, stepping into a dark foyer smelling of old rugs and disinfectant.

"Sure," she said, and disappeared down a dark hallway. "I'll just get him for you. Sit down, Billy. Sit down."

He knew from previous visits that a Victorian parlor lay just to the right of the entrance foyer. He walked in and peered out through a dirty window at the deserted street outside. He may as well be in New Jersey, he thought as he considered the spotless sidewalks and well-cared-for houses. All that was missing were the wrap-around lawns and two-car garages.

Brendan's hair was tousled with sleep. A pair of unbuttoned jeans clung precariously to his hips. His long bony feet were bare.

"I woke you up?"

"Sort of," Brendan said, reaching out to slap hands.

He didn't look like the same Brendan who inhabited the bare bachelor quarters on 16th Street. The transformation was similar to the one Billy had observed in people he visited in hospital. They were the same and yet somehow not the same, as if their environment and even the clothes they wore had as much to do with who they were as did their individual personalities.

"Want some coffee?"

Brendan led the way to the back of the old two-story house where a large kitchen had been added on. It looked out onto a dirt yard and was easily the house's brightest room despite an overhanging maple.

Brendan yawned mightily as Billy took a chair by the old oak table he remembered from when it was in the apartment on 16th Street. As Brendan went about heating up water and scratching, Billy watched for any sign of nerves that might indicate his friend had not been entirely truthful about his recent dealings with the police. The fact that Brendan hadn't yet shown any curiosity about this unexpected visit was reason enough for suspicion.

"I told my mother to wake me up at nine, but she pays no attention," Brendan said, lighting the gas and yawning again, this time less convincingly. "How'd you make out at the precinct?" he said, his back to the kitchen table.

"No problem," Billy said.

"They let you go just like that?"

"Sure. I couldn't help them out, they knew that. It was all just a formality."

"That's great, Billy. That's really great."

"By the way, Bren, how did you come to hear about them taking me in for questioning?"

Brendan abruptly turned toward the stove again.

"Rosemary told me. I saw her on the avenue and she said the bulls cuffed you on her stairway."

"News travels fast."

"That's for sure. Especially in that neighborhood. You want milk and sugar, right?"

Brendan poured boiling water into two chipped mugs he had set out on the table and fetched milk from the refrigerator. Then he sat down, yawned and shook himself like a wet dog.

"I was up all night plowing cunt. I thought my dick would fall off."

Billy sipped some coffee but said nothing. To the best of his knowledge, Brendan hadn't touched a woman in years.

"Tits like watermelons, swear to God."

Brendan laughed a just-among-us-boys laugh. Billy managed a smile.

"Picked her up in that bar on 86th Street. Know the one I mean? Christ, I haven't picked up nobody like that in a dog's age. She wanted to fuck in the natural, you know, no condom or nothing. Shit, I could get a fucking case of AIDS. I was drunk, but I wasn't *that* drunk."

"It's a good idea to be careful."

"Damn straight. I always carry a condom."

"Got to watch your back."

Brendan darted a glance his way, then looked back down at his coffee mug.

"You brought her back here?"

"What, are you nuts? My mother'd skin me alive. No way. We made it in the bushes by the Verrazano."

Billy recalled a brief encounter he once had with a senior from Immaculate Heart of Mary in the park under that bridge. He damned near froze his ass off in those bushes even though it was late May. That was all he remembered about the experience apart from some boat blowing its foghorn in the bay.

"Pretty chilly time of year for fucking in the bushes, Bren."

"Damn right. But this one was hot, Billy. I mean *hot*. I no more finish coming than she wants to do it again. Must be a nympho or something." He sipped some coffee, then asked, "So, what's next, Bill? The cops finished with you or what?"

"Gotta go back for a hearing. Some bullshit."

"But they didn't pin nothing on you, right? I mean, it was all routine and everything?"

"Sure, Bren, just routine. They thought they could tie me into that murder because Tommy McCready happened to give me a ride over to Ocean Parkway that night. But he dropped me off half an hour before they wasted the yam, so I'm clean."

"Is that right?"

"Him and a couple guidos was tooling down 16th Street and Tommy offered me a ride over to the Parkway. I didn't know nothing about where they was really headed. I got out of the car at the Parkway, and that was that. But I guess the cops figured I got a look at who was in the car. Only, I didn't. All I saw was the back of their heads. Except for Tommy. But the cops already knew Tommy was driving. They said he cooperated, and they sort of suggested it was Tommy told them I was in the car that night."

"Figures."

"Only, I know better."

"You do?"

128

Billy took a long sip of coffee, watching his friend's face carefully.

"Tommy got nothing to gain by fingering me. Suppose I did know the goons in the car? Suppose I was paying attention instead of looking at the scenery? That only means I could give the cops a description, and that would dig Tommy's grave even deeper."

"I see what you mean," Brendan said, although by the look on his face Billy could tell he didn't see anything, nor was he meant to. He had learned a long time ago that if you talked as if you understood something plainly, nine times out of ten the person you were talking to would play along rather than be thought too dimwitted to follow you.

"So I wasn't much help to the cops," Billy went on as Brendan contemplated the plastic tablecloth. Billy had not for a moment bought his story about making it with some girl in the bushes under the Verrazano. More likely, he had spent the evening in the Seven Two, then hightailed it to his mother's.

"By the way," he said as Brendan seemed to be come out of his brown study. "A green Bonneville followed me down the block earlier today. Tinted windows. They could of blown my brains out ten times over, so that ain't what they come for."

"That right?" Brendan said, wide-awake now.

"You better watch your ass, Bren. You can't tell what they might be up to."

# CHAPTER SEVENTEEN

For good measure, Billy dropped by the state employment office in Brooklyn Heights. Not surprisingly, they had nothing for a twenty-three-year-old high school dropout with no work history and an unorthodox way of expressing himself. He suggested that he and the interviewer, a young West Indian woman who hoped to make a good career out of civil service, should set up a business selling incense on subway platforms. He was told to report back in a month.

"Did you have any luck?" his mother asked when he returned home.

"Nope, nothing," he said, a salami sandwich in one hand, a Coke in the other. He was watching after-school cartoons on the old black-and-white she kept in the living room for her own use. There was a second, color TV in her daughter's room. Cathleen liked to watch television before going to sleep, and her mother would not hear of Cathleen doing without the color set.

"Maybe tomorrow you'll fare better," she said, bending down painfully to pick up crumbs from his sandwich. "Maybe Cath-a-leen could even find you something at her own firm. A nice clerical position. Something you could work your way up from."

She straightened up slowly and brushed the crumbs into a pot of philodendron.

"That's a possibility," he said, although he knew his sister would no more recommend him for a job where she worked than she would take him into the ladies room. "Any more bright ideas?" he added under his breath.

His mother approached the dilapidated sofa and touched his blond head. She rarely touched him since he had become full-grown, though when he was small they both used to delight in his sitting on her knee while she bounced him up and down and called him her apple dumpling.

"You're a good boy, Billy," she said, her eyes filling up with the memory of that small child. His transformation from child to adolescent and now manhood had left her confused. No longer able to cuddle him on her lap, her maternal feelings nonetheless persisted. He no longer approached her for a hug or kiss except on the most formal occasions, and she felt awkward about taking a grown man in her arms uninvited.

"Thanks, Ma," he said when he felt her hand on his head. He was used to women fondling him, and his mother's touch meant nothing more nor less than the touch of a stranger. "Can I make you a cup of tea or something?" he said, not taking his eyes off Tom and Jerry.

"No, thank you, dear," she replied in a sad voice. "Thanks just the same."

Despite a nap, two movies and a bunch of cartoons, there was still a major part of the day to get through, and he was already running low on "medication." Luckily, he had made sure Griswald checked the refill box on his prescription.

"Kind of a quick refill, ain't it, Billy?" the pharmacist said as he pushed the stapled white prescription bag toward him. He knew Billy from the days when he and Brendan used to shoplift jawbreakers out of the glass jars on the countertop. They had become so adept at it, the man couldn't catch them even though he knew what they were up to.

"Hand it over, Barney. I'm paying good American money."

The druggist accepted the ten dollars Billy had lifted out of his mother's pocketbook, but as he made change said, "I called up Doctor Griswald just to make sure he didn't make a mistake."

"Congratulations, Barney. I hope you get a medal."

"What'd you do, Billy, put a gun to his head?"

Billy was usually willing to match the pharmacist jibe for jibe, but today he didn't feel like prolonging the conversation. "I just told him your mother would come by to give him a blow job. What's the matter, Barney, you don't seem to enjoy dealing drugs like you used to."

He was halfway out of the store before the pharmacist finally found his voice.

"You stay the hell out of here!" he shouted, forgetting he had other customers.

Once out on the street again the idea of returning to his mother's darkening apartment seemed too depressing to contemplate. He bought a can of beer and downed two fresh amphetamines. Then he decided it was time to drop in on Rosemary.

He inserted a piece of plastic into the outer door to trip the lock and let himself into the dark foyer. The landlady was nowhere in sight, so he made his way up the dark stairway where he had been hand-cuffed a couple days earlier, and knocked gently on the door.

"Hello, Rosy, old girl."

She glanced up from an already overstuffed pail into which she was trying to cram yet another dirty diaper.

"Jesus Christ. Where'd you come from?"

She made another attempt at getting the lid back on, then gave up and, wiping her hands on the sides of her worn jeans, made a rush at him.

"God, I'm glad to see you," she said, pressing her mouth against his own.

"Is that why you had that welcoming committee waiting for me the other day?"

She was biting his earlobes and sucking on his neck, but the smell of diaper acted as a break on his lust.

"You know I would never do that to you, Billy Boy. Christ," she said, feeling for his crotch, "I been dying for you."

"Rosy, you ain't supposed to let no cops lay for me like that," he said, pushing her back. "You ain't supposed to let them put a gun to my head and take me away in cuffs."

"I never did, Billy," she said, opening his fly. "I swear to God, I didn't have no choice. They barged in and told me to keep my mouth shut or they'd take me in for soliciting."

"Is that right?" he said, starting to lose concentration.

She said something that he took to mean, "I swear to God!" then he was helping her pull down his pants. A child started to cry in the next room, but he heard it as if in a dream.

He left Rosemary's at quarter to six, letting her precede him down the dark staircase to listen at the landlady's door until the coast was clear. Then he slipped out into the first rush of commuters exiting the subway station. His stomach was growling—all she had in her ancient refrigerator were a half-quart of milk and some chocolate layer cake. His earlier fear of the Bonneville no longer seemed real. He had the familiar sense that he could cope with any situation thrown his way and, with half a dozen pills still left of his refill, he knew he would continue to feel this way for another twenty-four hours.

He found his mother lying on her narrow cot. She had a damp cloth on her head, a sign she was suffering from one of her migraines.

"What's for dinner?" he greeted her, although he knew the answer would be a frown. "Another headache?" he called from the nearby kitchen, making do with a soda until he could cajole her into fixing him something.

She swallowed slowly and nodded.

"You took aspirin?"

Another nod, this time setting off a flash of anger in him. Suddenly he felt fed up with this hypochondriac woman and the smell of her dirty, dilapidated apartment. He wanted to walk out of it for good, go west and start a real life for himself, far away from the suffering saint who had borne him and now seemed a continual reproach to his existence. He had heard that when you moved to a new place where nobody knew you it was like beginning life all over again. That seemed exactly what he needed.

"Your sister called," she barely whispered.

"That right?"

"She'll be late. That's why I haven't started supper," she said, raising her hand toward her brow like a silent-movie actress. Supper was an early affair in the Conover house. It was originally planned that way so that food would be on the table when his father got home from work. Billy was surprised to find that other people ate at seven or even eight o'clock, an hour in his childhood when he was already getting ready for bed. Now a grown man, his stomach still ached for a plate of baked or broiled meat with a boiled potato and vegetable at the same time it did when he was a kid.

"Can't you at least get it started? I ain't had nothing all day."

His mother took a long, uneven breath. For a moment she looked as if she were going to cry but, with an effort, pushed herself up from the old cot.

"That's all I'm good for. An old workhorse. Keep pushing till it dies."

He paid no attention. He had been hearing the same complaints for as far back as he could remember, though in fact they only began after his father's death. He went into the living room and turned on the evening news. He watched victims of a multiple murder in the South Bronx get loaded into ambulances and listened to eyewitness accounts of the "drug-related" slaying. Then he watched with equal interest a commercial for low-fat margarine that tasted exactly like butter. This was followed by the latest developments in a love-triangle murder and some footage of a deaf-mute demonstration on the steps of City Hall. There was nothing about the Flatbush killing.

After a while he could smell some kind of meat baking and felt his stomach rumble again. Usually amphetamines acted as a brake on his appetite. He had gone for entire days without eating, living off sodas and potato chips and feeling none the worse until the pills wore off.

"When's it gonna be ready?" he called, noting it was already half an hour past their usual mealtime. For answer, he heard a pot hit the iron grates on top of the stove. A minute later his mother came into the room and said, "Your sister called to say she'll be late. We'll eat when she gets here."

"We can't eat before that?"

"I don't have the strength to make two meals, Billy. Try to show some consideration."

"But I'm starving."

"Eat bread and butter."

"I don't want bread and butter. I want supper."

"You'll have it soon enough."

He mumbled an obscenity and turned back to the TV where a beached whale was being pushed back into the surf by some people on the Jersey shore.

"How come she's late? Cath-a-leen's never late."

"I can't tell you, Billy."

"Let her get her own dinner."

"That's not how we do things in this house, young man. Cath-a-leen works hard. Where would we be without her? You know I couldn't afford to pay the rent on what the government gives me."

"Yeah, yeah."

"And I don't see you out earning no money."

"That's right, Ma. And you sure know where to stick the knife."

"Well, that's not what I meant," she added in a more conciliatory tone. "But you shouldn't be so ungrateful for what Cath-a-leen does for us." She paused to stare at a quartet of dancing hubcaps on the TV screen. "It would be different if your father was alive."

The mention of his father silenced him.

"If Daddy was still with us, I could do a lot of things I can't do now."

"Okay, Ma. Forget it."

"Don't you think I'd like to take a little vacation now and then? Do you think I wouldn't like that?"

"I said forget it."

"Or maybe even buy a car. Just to take a day trip once in a while. Over to Jersey. Maybe go shopping at a mall."

"Fuck!" he cried, thrashing his legs the way he did when he was six years old, making contact with an end table holding a vase which predated his own entry into the world. The table went flying across the room. The vase remained behind, dropping like a stone to the frayed carpet and splitting into three neat pieces.

"Now look what you've done!"

The entrance door to the apartment swung open.

"Is that you, Cath-a-leen?" his mother called. Then, as if both her children were fifteen years younger, she said, "Come and see what your brother's just done."

Billy got up and stomped down the long corridor toward his sister's room. She had already disappeared inside and closed the door behind her.

"Sis, can I see you a minute?"

There was no answer.

"Can I come in, Cath-a-leen?"

He tried the knob and found it unlocked. She was lying face-down on the baby-blue coverlet, her street clothes still on, a black pump dangling from one foot.

Entering his sister's room always seemed like entering another world. The rest of the house was dirty, dark and ancient. But in here it was a page out of a storybook. The walls were papered with a pattern of tiny purple flowers. The floor was covered by a shag rug. On the wall at the foot of the bed was a Bruce Springsteen poster. A girl's desk, the oldest object in the room—Cathleen had had it since she was in elementary school—stood against the wall opposite her bed. This was how her home would look one day. Not just her bedroom, but every room in the house, just like his aunts' houses, with everything clean and tidy. He couldn't imagine living in such a place.

"You okay, Sis?"

"Yes," she said into the pillow.

"How come you're stretched out? You tired or something?"

"Yes, I'm tired."

"Listen, I could use a couple dollars. I just broke Ma's vase, the one Grandma gave her. It was an accident, but she's pitching a bitch and I don't feel like hanging around to listen. I promise I'll pay you back. What d'you say?"

He let it all out in one breath, not feeling optimistic about his chances. That he was speaking the truth, more or less, made him feel even less confident than if he were making up a story.

"Take it from my bag."

He had already noted her handbag on top of the desk. He hesitated—she had never let him so much as touch her purse before—then undid the clasp and fished around inside until he found her wallet.

"I'm just taking five," he said, removing a ten as he glanced over his shoulder. She hadn't moved. He added some ones, then closed the purse and put it back on the desk. "I'll pay this back, don't worry," he said, reaching for the doorknob.

She didn't reply.

# CHAPTER EIGHTEEN

His first stop was the Chinese take-out next to Scully's. He sometimes stopped by there to hit on the girls behind the counter. He liked Chinese women despite their small breasts. But the help never gave him the slightest encouragement.

He ordered fried rice and shrimp—not the dinner he had had in mind an hour ago—and carried it to a table next to the big plate-glass window.

Before it became a Chinese take-out that location was occupied by a driving school and before that by a kids' clothing store. Stores in the neighborhood were opening and closing faster than he could keep track of. The take-out attracted a young working crowd, not just locals but new people, tall slim girls with big boobs and young men who dressed like movie actors from the 1930s. Many of them lived together without benefit of clergy, which in Billy's eyes meant the women were fair game. Some were willing enough to talk to him, but they invariably turned the conversation in other directions when he tried to get personal. Still, he liked the way they carried themselves with a sure jaunty step so unlike the drag-ass girls from the neighborhood.

The rice and shrimp—the only Chinese food he ever ate—was supposed to be much better than what used to be served at the take-out that preceded this one across the street. But he scarcely noticed the difference, content merely to fill up the huge cavity in his stomach. As he ate he watched the other customers or gazed out the window at commuters on their way home.

"Rosy!"

He jumped up and darted toward the door, causing two of the

male cooks to rush toward the front of the store, chopping knives in hand.

"Rosy, old girl!"

She had almost reached the corner of 16th Street. When she saw who was calling after her, she reluctantly retraced her steps, her cutoff jeans, chosen originally to show off a comely rear, now straining the denim to its limit.

"Can't stop, Billy. I left the kids alone."

"Come on in the chinks and have a bite."

"I'd like to. But they'll burn the house down as sure as shootin'."

"Just for a minute. We never get a chance to see each other outside that rathole of yours. The change'll do you good."

He bought a second order of fried rice and put it down in front of her. For all her demurring, she began to eat greedily. "I ain't had nothing since breakfast. I ain't even been out of that house in weeks except to run to the store."

"You need to get out more often, Rosy. Enjoy yourself a bit."

"Easy for you to say. Who do I get to baby-sit? My landlady? She hates kids. Though I can't say as how I blame her. I wouldn't want to be stuck with one if I wasn't already."

"You make motherhood sound like something less than a noble vocation."

"Fuck motherhood. If I had half a brain I woulda had abortions. I let my mother talk me into having the first. The second I got nobody to blame but myself."

"So maybe it really is a calling," he said, glancing appreciatively at the big breasts swinging beneath her stained T-shirt. "We all have our callings."

"Right. What's yours, Billy? Second-story jobs?"

He glanced around apprehensively.

"You don't know nothing about that, Rosy. One more slip of the tongue and my ass could end up in Attica. As it is, I'm only out on the street through the good graces of a certain detective in the Seven Two."

Then, in a normal voice, he added, "It's like the Gospel says—some of us is Marthas and some is Marys."

"Maybe you should keep that in mind the next time you can't keep your dick inside your pants. Has it ever occurred to you maybe I wouldn't have two brats if it wasn't for that wiener of yours?"

He had never imagined for a moment that either of her children could be the product of his own lust. Or, at the very least, that anyone with Rosemary's morals could determine who among her paramours and various clientele was responsible for a particular pregnancy.

"Surely you exaggerate," he said.

"Exaggerate, my ass. Ain't you ever took a good look at him? If he ain't your kid, then I'm a monkey's uncle," she said, licking her fingers. "You gonna eat the rest of your rice?"

He found himself at a loss for a comeback. Fatherhood was a serious matter. He alternately venerated and hated his own dead father. He had never personally considered what fatherhood would be like for himself, never imagined he could *be* a father. He didn't know what to make of this strange new feeling, confused as it was with the smell of peanut oil and the eau de diaper pail Rosemary emanated.

"I ain't never said nothing about it," she said, scraping the last few grains of rice off her plate, "but I thought it must be pretty obvious if you just took a look at the kid. I mean, everybody on the block could tell he's yours even if I never opened my mouth."

"Did you? Open your mouth?"

"No," she said. "I mean, it ain't nobody else's business, right?"

"Right."

"I get the Welfare and everything, so I don't ask you for nothing. But I figured you knowed."

She couldn't realize it, but his relationship to her had just radically changed. Even her physical appearance seemed to have altered: The appealing breasts beneath that soiled T-shirt bore the nipples that had suckled his son, though she had actually bottle-fed both her children. Those broad hips were the vehicle that had borne and discharged the boy into the world.

Suddenly the idea of her dawdling over the remains of a greasy meal while her child, *his* child, had been left alone in an apartment prey to God-knew-what dangers, was out of the question.

"Rosy, get your ass home. You don't leave kids by themselves. They could burn the fucking house down."

He put his hand under the fleshy part of her arm and urged her toward the door.

"I ain't finished eating."

"Off you go. And if what you told me's true, I don't want you leaving them kids alone again, no matter what. You understand?"

"Ain't you getting pretty bossy all of a sudden?" she said as he ushered her rapidly down the avenue.

"And I'm telling you something else: I don't want you taking no drugs when you're around them. Any drugs you take, you take with me. Otherwise nothing, *nada*. You got that?"

"Who appointed you parish priest?"

"I did. Priest of your parish."

As they rounded the corner of 16th Street, the usual crowd in and outside Scully's watched with interest as the two neighborhood icons, one more disreputable than the other, conducted what looked like a typical marital tiff.

"Does that mean you're gonna start playing daddy?" she said, doing double-time to keep up with him.

"You better believe it. I'm coming by every day from now on. So you better stay on your toes."

"I guess that also means you're also gonna start contributing to your son's upkeep. Not to mention putting away something for his college education."

He blushed to think the kind of life he had been living when his own flesh and blood—his father's grandson—had been left to the care of a part-time whore.

"That's right," he said, "it does."

By the time they reached the gate of the areaway to her building, she too had undergone a change. In response to what she had merely meant as an offhand remark, Billy had shown a side to himself she could never have guessed at. It was a revelation that enhanced his already proven attractiveness.

"How about coming upstairs for a quickie?"

"No time, Rosy. I'll stop by in the morning after I see about a job downtown."

"You really gonna get a job?"

"In the meantime, see to it that Little Billy has everything he needs. If he don't, you let me know. And, Rosy?" he said, raising a finger in her face the same as his father used to do, "I *don't* want you turning no more tricks."

He had originally intended to find someone with an extra joint, but now he didn't even remember why he had left his mother's apartment. He was obsessed with his newly discovered paternity, with trying to get used to the feeling of it, a kind of numbness in that part of his brain that was usually so agitated. For as far back as could remember, but actually only since his ninth year, his mind had been in a nearly continuous buzz. Before he started using drugs there seemed to be no relief for it. When he discovered pot and amphetamines he thought he had made friends for life. Only gradually did he learn that no matter how good drugs made him feel, he would never lead a normal life like other kids. But by that point he was no longer sure he wanted to. Being a freak had made him disdainful of normalcy and made him embrace his pariah state and the nonconformist lifestyle it offered not as a curse but as his fate, for better or worse. But it was a fate that rarely let him have a moment's peace—certainly not the kind of focused calm he was feeling this particular spring evening.

He looked up and down 16th Street like someone who had never been there before. He was amazed to find the trees behind the senior citizen's high-rise sprouting bright green leaves. Then he discovered that the smaller, more recently planted maples by the curbsides were also in bloom. They didn't look like this every spring, did they? How could he have missed them? Even the play of the streetlight on the parked cars and sidewalks seemed beautiful, as if deliberately designed for the effect. Maybe he was just experiencing some kind of withdrawal. Maybe all this beauty was just some kind of chemical imbalance, setting him up for an another confrontation with the terrible void. On the other hand, maybe his life had finally taken a turn out of the junkyard.

"Ma?"

He found her stretched out on the living room sofa, a damp cloth on her head.

"Another headache?"

She nodded.

"Ma, I'm sorry I broke your vase. I'm sorry I spoke back to you. I won't do it again."

Her only reaction was a twitch above one eyebrow.

"You and Cath-a-leen ate?" he said.

"I saved dinner," she whispered as if she were ready for the last rites. "In the oven with a piece of foil on top."

"Thanks. I'll have it later."

He turned and walked down the long corridor. His sister's door was closed. He knocked, got no response, then turned the knob and opened it a few inches. Cathleen was lying in the same position he had left her in an hour ago. She still hadn't changed out of her work clothes.

"You okay?"

She buried her head in the pillow.

"I brought back your change. I accidentally took more than I meant to."

He opened her pocketbook and returned the money he had taken earlier minus what he had spent in the Chinese take-out.

"You ain't sick or nothing? You don't usually lay around in your clothes all night."

He looked for a clue to explain why she was feeling so bad, but all he saw were the raincoat she hadn't bothered to hang up and some kind of plastic bag she must have brought home with her. He picked up the coat, causing the bag to fall to the floor. At the sound his sister turned over, then quickly got up and snatched the coat from him. It happened so quickly he barely had time to glimpse a clump of gauze that had started to fall out of the plastic, some of it stained red.

"I was only gonna hang it up."

"Never mind," she said, clutching the bag to her breast. "Just leave me alone. Who said you could just barge in here?"

She was trying to sound angry but didn't seem to have the energy for it.

"Why don't you tell me what happened, Sis?"

"Nothing happened."

"Then, how come you didn't bother to change out of your work clothes? How come you didn't hang up your coat? You always hang up your coat."

"I'm tired, that's all. I'm not feeling well."

"I seen you sick before and you never acted like this." He sat down on the bed beside her. "You can talk to me, Cath-a-leen."

She was still clutching the plastic bag as if there were something valuable inside. Her bottom lip started to quiver. This was how she used to look when he teased her—not knowing, never knowing, if he was for real. Her only defense was to assume that he was never sincere and so always to be on guard.

"I'll be fine if I just get some rest."

"You had dinner?"

She nodded.

"When you're feeling better I got something I want to tell you."

"Tell me."

He had thought he would make the announcement matter-of-factly, but when it came down to it he found himself pleasurably embarrassed. He had not had any good news to announce to his family since the day he won a merit badge in the Scouts shortly before being thrown out of the troop.

"I'm a daddy."

She turned toward him and frowned. "You're a what?"

"Rosemary Grady's boy. I'm his father."

She searched his face, trying to see if he was pulling her leg. But then her frown dissolved and her eyes widened. She gave a cry like an old woman who had just been told about a death in the family, and fell back on the bed.

# CHAPTER NINETEEN

He spent the rest of the evening at home, watching TV with his mother and wondering what would be her reaction if he told her she had a grandson. He let her warm up the dinner she had made earlier, then fixed a cup of tea for her while she watched the ten o'clock news.

Meanwhile, Cathleen fell asleep in her clothes. At least, that was what Billy told his mother after she sent him to look in on his sister. At first, Cathleen really did seem to be sleeping, but when he passed by her door a little later he thought he heard crying. He recalled that she sometimes got testy or depressed when she was getting her period, and then remembered the stained gauze he had seen. It was only later in the evening, while he was waiting to hear if there were any further developments in the murder case, that he remembered she was supposed to be pregnant. He didn't know a lot about how the female reproductive system worked, but he was pretty sure pregnant women didn't get periods—not if everything was going as it was supposed to.

He slipped away during the weather report on the pretense of getting a soda and let himself into Cathleen's room again. This time she really was sleeping, her mouth hung open the same as when they were little and took naps together. He looked around for the plastic bag she had guarded so closely, but it was nowhere in sight. He looked in the waste basket under her desk, but it wasn't there either. Finally, he checked the bedspread she had partially pulled over herself and spotted it under the fringe of the coverlet. He removed it carefully, noticing her sleep was deeper than a mid-evening nap. Then he saw a prescription bottle on the bed beside her. The label identified it as a strong painkiller dentists sometimes prescribed.

"Jesus Christ, Cath-a-leen," he said under his breath. He put the bag back on the bed and counted the pills to make sure she hadn't exceeded the recommended dosage. Then he let himself out of the room and headed for the kitchen to get his soda. He picked one at random and just as absentmindedly opened it.

"Jesus fucking Christ."

Had he stayed near the television he would have heard the DA announce he would be asking for the indictments of two more of the perpetrators in the Flatbush slaying within the next couple days. Mrs. Conover hadn't really understood what her son had been charged with and so didn't consider the item newsworthy enough to pass along to him when he returned. Instead she repeated the weather report— mild spring temperatures with a chance of thundershowers in the afternoon.

The next morning he was up with the first sounds of activity in the house. He found Cathleen in the kitchen making coffee.

"How's it going?" he said.

"What gets you up so early?"

He poured some coffee—no one but Cathleen took the trouble to brew it fresh—and sat down at the table.

"Job hunting," he said, watching her apply her makeup with the help of a small mirror attached to the kitchen wall.

She gave him a sidelong glance from beneath her eyebrow pencil.

"Well, I got responsibilities now."

"Before this you didn't?"

"Not the same thing."

She smiled sardonically, with no trace of the anguish she had seemed to feel the previous evening. "You're absolutely sure it's yours? I mean, nothing personal, Billy, but Rosemary Grady doesn't exactly have a reputation for being the Virgin Mary."

"I know that."

"How old is it?"

"Three," he said, though he wasn't really sure.

"How come she kept it a secret so long?" She gave him a quick glance, then applied a coat of lipstick to her nicely formed mouth.

"I guess she didn't want to cause no trouble."

"What do you two do now, get married and live happily ever after?"

145

"You don't approve?"

She snapped her makeup case shut.

"I don't care if you marry the cat's first cousin. I'll still have to look after Mom, won't I?"

"Maybe I could help."

"How? By bringing her to live with you and Rosemary?"

"I mean after I get a job."

"A job?"

"Like I said, now I got responsibilities. By the way, they wouldn't be looking for somebody at your office? Like in the stockroom, maybe, or maintenance?"

"Not likely."

After she left he walked to the corner and bought a copy of the *News*. He figured a guard job would be in his line. He knew all the tricks of the thieving trade, so he should be able to spot funny business pretty easily. But then he recalled most guard jobs involved a security check.

A factory in Greenpoint was looking for assemblers. The starting salary was minimum wage. He could do better than that.

He decided to try the merchants along 9th Avenue. There were two small supermarkets, a couple delis and two pizzerias. He could do stock work, make deliveries, anything just to start bringing in some money. If he didn't have a pay stub to show the next time he appeared in court, the judge could remand him to Riker's. That was a prospect that just a day earlier would not have seemed half as bad as it did this morning. A year away from women was painful but possible. A year away from the son he barely knew suddenly seemed like an eternity.

He made a sincere pitch to the owner of the supermarket next to the all-night deli, a Russian Jew who once threw him out of the store for shoplifting. He told Billy there was no opening. When Billy persisted, the man threatened to call the police.

Next he tried the other supermarket two blocks further up the avenue. The owner and he were less well-acquainted, but the man knew him by reputation. He didn't threaten to call the police, but he was firm and eventually Billy left.

Next he tried the delis. The kids behind the counters told him he would have to come back and talk to the owners.

Finally he approached the first of the pizzerias, a new sit-down place run by an Italian immigrant who used to operate out of a hole-in-the-wall a block away. They knew each other from when Billy used to come in for an ice when he was barely tall enough to reach the counter. The man had just opened up for the day and was getting ready for the lunchtime rush.

"Hey, Joe, whad'ya know?" Billy said. "How's business?"

"So so," Joe said, rolling up the corrugated iron gate which had been spray-painted by local graffiti artists.

"Good enough to take on a little extra help?"

The gate got stuck halfway up, giving Billy a chance to lend a hand. Joe thanked him matter-of-factly and unlocked the door. Billy was steeling himself for yet another rejection when, having wedged the front door of the store open, the owner said, "For you?"

"Who else? I could do deliveries or work behind the counter, what-ever you like."

"I got plenty help behind the counter. But I got nobody make lunch delivery. I been making myself. But that's no good because I gotta leave the store just when it gets busy."

The man checked the canned sodas in the refrigerator cases, then said, "You could work middle of the day?"

"Sure. I can work anytime."

"You could start today, now?"

"Sure," Billy said, his heart speeding up as it hadn't done since he pulled his last burglary. "I can start right this minute."

At 2:00 p.m. the pizza man handed him a ten-dollar bill and told him, "You come back tomorrow, you make another."

Billy thanked him and pocketed the money. Then he headed straight for Rosemary's apartment. He rang the bell and waited for the old landlady to appear. When she croaked something unfriendly at him he said, "I'm here to see my son," she opened the door without another word.

Rosemary had just finished bathing the two kids, the older of which was running about the house wet and naked. Even to Billy's untrained eye the place looked cleaner than it had the day before. The garbage was no longer overflowing with banana peels and empty soup cans. The oilcloth looked as if it might have received a washing. And Rose-mary herself lacked some of the baggy-eyed hang-dog look he had come to expect.

"I got a job," he said.

"Where?"

"Frank's. I only make deliveries and help out during the noon rush. But it's a start. Here," he said, digging into his jeans until he came up with the ten dollars Frank had paid him. He still had another seven which he had made on tips. "Get the kid some clothes or something."

Rosemary regarded the money as if it were currency from some exotic land, then stuffed it into the left cup of her bra.

"Speaking of the kid," she said, pulling a T-shirt over the younger child's head with the vehemence of a short-tempered cop taking somebody into custody, "you think you can keep an eye on him while I run this one over to the avenue for a new pair of shoes?"

Billy had never come any closer to childcare than playing skalzies with kids on the street. But he shrugged and said, "Sure. You got coffee in the house?"

"In the refrigerator," she said, working on a pair of knotted shoelaces. "We'll be back in half an hour. It's nap time, but he'll probably wait till I get back. Don't let him get into trouble."

"Don't worry," he said, searching for the coffee amid a rubble of wilted lettuce and three sticky half-empty jars of grape jelly.

Rosemary hastily applied some lipstick. On her way out she again cautioned Billy to keep a close eye on the boy, who was playing with a toy hammer on the floor.

Billy turned on the gas under a metal saucepan full of water for his coffee. Then he watched his son hammer an imaginary nail into the kitchen floor, talking to himself or an imaginary companion.

"Hey, champ, how's it going?"

The boy ignored this first attempt to parley and continued with his carpentry. But the dialogue he was carrying on became more animated and his hammerings more purposeful.

Billy squatted down so as to get closer to eye level and frog-walked closer to the boy.

"Hey, Billy, what's up?"

The boy looked up, his face softening as if in recognition. Encouraged, Billy sat down beside him.

"What're you working on? A house?"

The boy mumbled something and struck the linoleum forcefully.

"Skyscraper?"

The boy struck the floor again, mouthed some garbled words, then looked up again at the stranger in whose charge he had been left.

"Want me to help?"

Billy stretched out his hand to take the toy hammer. The boy smiled broadly, causing Billy to break into a wide grin himself, flushed with the success of this first attempt to strike up a relationship. Then the boy raised the hammer high over his head and brought it down sharply on his father's head.

"You...son-of-a-bitch!"

The boy set up a howl of mean-spirited laughter. Billy wrenched the hammer from him and threw it out the open kitchen window. The boy's laughter turned to wails of outrage. He lunged at his father's leg and sank his two new teeth into it.

When Rosemary returned home father and son were sitting at opposite ends of the kitchen like two cellmates who had just tried to kill each other.

"You two got along okay?"

"He tried to bash my brains in with his fucking hammer."

"I hope you took it away from him."

"I threw it out the fucking window."

"Jesus Christ. I thought I was leaving an adult in charge."

"That kid needs to learn manners."

"Maybe if he had a man around he would."

"Don't worry, I'll teach him. If I don't kill him first."

# CHAPTER TWENTY

He was on his way out of Rosemary's building and, despite his sore forehead, feeling better about himself than he had in years, when a blue and white police car appeared at the curbside. A half second later a cop was manacling his wrists.

"I don't believe this. I already spoke with Detective McCaffrey. I seen the DA and everything."

But the cops, neither of whom he recognized, told him he was under arrest for the murder of Andrew Mott, read him his rights and put him into the backseat of the patrol car.

"I tell you, you're making a mistake," he said as they drove away. "I already copped a plea. I been arraigned, for Christ sake."

The two cops said nothing until they were halfway to the station house and Billy had repeated his protest twice more. Finally the driver, a youth not much older than his prisoner, said, "What's the matter, Billy, you don't read the papers or watch TV?"

"What papers? What TV? I don't know what you're talking about."

But the cop only shook his head and made a hard left turn onto Fourth Avenue. For the rest of the trip Billy got nothing more out of them.


"It's a whole new ballgame," the Assistant District Attorney told him.

"What do you mean? We got a deal, don't we?"

"Not any more. Not since two people fingered you as the shooter."

"What the fuck you talking about? I didn't even get out of the car. I didn't even know where they were going."

"Two people, Billy. Two people say you pulled the trigger. Against

150

your say-so you didn't. Plus your fingerprints all over the murder weapon."

"And how many other prints besides? I told you, the guido—I mean, the Italian guy," he said, judging by the cut of the ADA's suit, his haircut and last name that he was probably Italian, "the guy who killed the yam gave the piece to Tommy McCready. Tommy passed it to me when I got out of the car. He told me to bury it, which I did. The other two meatheads can back up what I say."

"Nobody's backing up nobody, Billy. You're on your own now."

Billy stared hard at the young lawyer. He knew this kind of questioning was probably a ploy, a bargaining position. He also knew he had a right to his own attorney.

"Maybe I should talk to my lawyer. You guys can't be trusted anymore than those bozos in the car."

"That's your right, Billy. We never said you couldn't have a lawyer."

"I mean, I cooperated with you guys. I got goons in a Bonneville cruising my block. But I cooperated with youse. And now you come up with this shit."

"It's a pretty tight case, Billy. Two solid witnesses."

"Pillars of the fucking community."

"Against your word."

Billy took a deep, exasperated breath.

"So what do you want now? You wanna squeeze my balls a little harder? Okay, squeeze."

The ADA opened the middle button of his freshly pressed suit and leaned halfway across the table separating them.

"You give us a confession, we make a deal."

"A confession to murder?"

The ADA nodded.

"You gotta be out of your mind." He sat back, his heart beating hard. "I wanna see a lawyer."

He knew most Legal Aid attorneys were fresh out of law school and not good for much besides plea-bargaining. But he believed he would pretty much manage his own case anyway. Even so, when they called him down from his cell later that day to interview his lawyer, he had immediate doubts that the man assigned to him would be capable of getting a judge's attention, never mind pleading a case.

Ira Greenberg was five foot two and looked to weigh about as much as most ten-year-olds. Even his hand felt like a child's when Billy shook it.

"It looks like we've got our work cut our for us," Greenberg said cheerfully, opening a battered briefcase which looked a generation older than its owner. "The DA is talking Murder One. With any luck we can get him to come down to Man Two."

"Man Two?" Billy objected, causing the attorney to regard him cautiously over the tops of his rimless glasses. "I didn't shoot nobody, Ira. I'm fucking innocent."

"You're not interested in a plea bargain?"

"I just told you, man. I didn't kill nobody. I didn't even know what was going down until it was all over. I was—you should pardon the expression—just along for the ride."

Ira scratched his chin meditatively.

"I was under the impression this would be a plea bargain."

"No way."

"You realize if you're convicted you could get twenty-five-to-life?"

"I realize I didn't kill nobody, Mr. Greenberg. I realize all I did was go for what I thought would be a little ride with my old chum Tommy McCready, and the next thing I know the guy up front is blowing some black guy's brains out. That's all I know."

Ira regarded Billy as if had just said he was his first cousin, once-removed. Then his eyes lit up with a kind of interior combustion. He reached for his briefcase and pulled out a blank yellow pad, then fumbled inside his crumpled suit for a pen.

"Let's start from the beginning."

There was no question of Billy's making bail. He would be locked up in the Brooklyn House of Detention for as long as it took to come to trial. Thanks to the publicity surrounding the case, that wouldn't be as long as it might otherwise have been. But the prospect of even a couple weeks without freedom or any human contact except what was afforded by the other inmates of the NYC Department of Corrections, eating bad food, drinking stale coffee and, most important of all, without access to drugs, was not something he looked forward to.

He was put in with another white man, supposedly to minimize the chances of prison justice replacing the more orthodox kind. That was okay with Billy. What was not okay was the mate they chose for him. Arthur Rawson was under indictment for dealing in child pornography, a charge he passionately denied the one and only time Billy brought up the subject. Rawson said the material that was found in his apartment—a collection of movies, videotapes and stacks of glossy magazines—had been left there by a neighbor for safekeeping.

Billy spent most of his time reading—news magazines and mystery novels—and sleeping. Life was much more varied in a real prison, Rawson assured him. There you had daily outdoor exercise, a job of some kind and better food. Billy said he would gladly forgo those perks for the sake of the old sofa in his mother's living room.

His lawyer visited him three times the first week of his incarceration. But for the next several days Billy heard nothing from him. To pass the time he began reading law books, which were in great demand by other prisoners as well, and started to acquire a basic understanding of the philosophy as well as procedures of the judicial system. By the time Ira Greenberg turned up again, his client was full of questions about motions, rules of evidence and even more arcane legal matters.

"Suppose you leave all that to me," Ira told him. "What you should be worrying about is whether Tommy McCready will testify on your behalf."

"Why wouldn't he? I would testify to save his ass."

"Not if it meant sending your own there instead."

"Tommy's made a deal to lie under oath?"

"I've seen stranger things happen," Ira said, still, apart from a persistent five o'clock shadow, looking as if his time in a courtroom scarcely amounted to a couple months since law school.

"Which leaves me where?"

"Which leaves *us*," the lawyer said, opening his battered satchel, "relying on the testimony of the black kids who witnessed the shooting."

"To testify for me?"

"They have nothing to lose. Nobody's looking to make any deals with them—at least not as far as I can tell."

"You talked to them?"

"Somebody from my office has. I should know in a day or two

whether we can build a case around what they say."

Billy sat back on the slippery wooden chair and shook his head.

"I don't want to tell you your business, Ira, but I don't see why some black kid should stick his neck out to save mine. Not after I was with the guys who wasted their buddy."

"I admit it's a long shot. But it's the only one we have. The DA has two witnesses to the killing—alleged witnesses. They both put the gun in your hands."

"I never touched the piece till Tommy handed it to me."

"If they testify under oath, who's the jury going to believe, you or them?"

"And the guido who actually pulled the trigger?"

Ira pulled out a rap sheet from his briefcase, pushed his glasses up to his forehead and brought the piece of paper to within a few inches of his eyes.

"Two arrests for possession of firearms. No convictions."

"There you go. Two gun arrests. I never fired a gun in my life."

"Non-admissible evidence. Those arrests won't have any relevance to this case."

"The jury won't know about them?"

"If I mention them, the judge will start the trial all over again with a new jury."

"Jesus Christ. And they call this the 'justice' system?"

"That's how it works, Billy. Those two black kids are the best chance we've got. If the jury believes them—assuming they actually did see who pulled the trigger—we at least have reasonable doubt. If not..."

"...my ass is grass."

"It's not too late to plea-bargain to Manslaughter."

Billy regarded the young lawyer carefully.

"What would you say my chances are, Ira?"

"Fifty-fifty. That's if those black kids saw anything *and* are willing to testify."

"Can't they be forced to?"

"Sure, they can be compelled to take the stand. But they can't be compelled to say what we'd like them to say."

Billy took a deep breath and considered briefly whether lunch would again consist of cold franks and beans. Then he said, "I'll take my chances. I'm fucking innocent."

That afternoon his sister showed up for visiting hour. So did Rosemary Grady, in cut-off shorts and a tank top two sizes too small. He had no choice but to see them together, which meant he could not speak freely to either.

"How you feeling, Sis?"

"Fine," she said in a tone that stopped any further inquiry.

"How's little Billy?" he asked Rosemary.

"Okay. Full of the devil."

"He needs a crack on the ass now and then. Just a tap. How's Ma taking it?" he asked Cathleen.

"How would you expect? She sees you on TV being led into the courthouse in handcuffs. How do you think that makes a mother feel?"

"I'm innocent. You tell her that."

"I'll tell her."

"My lawyer offered me a plea bargain. I told him to stuff it."

"You think that's a good idea?" Rosemary said. "I mean, if you want to see your kid grow up, you can't do it from behind bars."

"Rosy," he replied, leaning toward the glass partition separating them, "I didn't kill nobody. I didn't fucking touch nobody even."

"Okay, Billy. I was just trying to help."

"Thanks. But what I need is for those other clowns to tell the truth when they get on the stand. That's what's gonna help."

"I asked at work," Cathleen said, "about this fellow representing you."

"Greenberg."

"Nobody ever heard of him."

"He's just starting out."

"Of course, the firm I work for doesn't do criminal law."

"They got other things on their mind," he said with a meaningful look. Rosemary watched their interchange but didn't know what to make of it.

After he returned to his cell he realized he didn't feel as confident about his decision to go to trial as he had made out to his visitors. He knew innocent people went to prison. But he also knew that if he copped a plea for a crime he didn't commit, the real killer would go free. That fact alone would gall him for the rest of his life. There was no way he could do five years in the slammer for somebody else's crime.

The next day he had a different kind of visitor.

"You take the rap, there's fifty big ones for you when you come out."

"Fifty grand for five years of my life?" Billy replied to the fire-plug in a dark suit. "Fifty thousand dollars to spend five years with a bunch of spades and butt-fuckers? That works out to what?—about thirty dollars a day. Even a street hoo-er can do better than that, and she don't have to be locked up in a cell all day."

"What would you consider a fair price?" the man asked, picking his teeth..

"How about half a mil?"

"Half a mil's pretty steep."

"So's five years in Attica."

"I'll have to talk it over with my boss."

"Why don't you do that?"

His cellmate drove him crazy with sex talk. For somebody who insisted so vehemently he was innocent, the man certainly had an intimate knowledge of the subject.

"Man, I seen a flick where this broad was getting it on with a St. Bernard and a Great Dane at the same time. The St. Bernard was humping her from behind and the Great Dane was humping the St. Bernard," he said with laugh that sent shivers through Billy.

He continued to read law books borrowed from the prison library. When he wanted a change of pace he read comics, tales about ordinary men turned into super-heroes by exposure to radiation or some freak accident. The comics were passed from cell to cell until they fell apart. By the time a newcomer got one, it was in shreds. But comics were better than nothing and they helped keep his mind off more serious matters.

A couple days later he got another visit from his attorney.

"Good news. McCready may be willing to testify if I can get him a plea that involves minimum jail time. It won't be easy, but it's a shot."

Billy didn't mention the fifty grand he had been offered. If, on the outside chance he did decide to accept some big bucks for his silence, that would be no business of Ira's.

"What about the other two who know I'm innocent—not counting the actual killer, of course?"

"Not so easy," Ira said, shaking his small, shaggy head as he rummaged through his briefcase. "Both of them are personal friends of the killer. That leaves your friend McCready."

"*Ex*-friend. Tommy's probably the bastard who fingered me in the first place."

"Maybe, maybe not. It doesn't matter now. The battle lines are drawn, with you and maybe Tommy on one side, and Bruno and his pals on the other. It'll be their word against yours."

"That's not such bad odds."

"Plus," the lawyer said, finally locating what he was looking for in his bag, "the murder weapon on which they found your prints, don't forget."

"Along with a few other people's."

"But not the murderer's. He's not so dumb if he thought to wipe them off before he handed the gun to Tommy to get rid of."

"It sounds like the bastard planned to hang it all on me right from the git-go."

"He very well might have."

Billy admired good planning. He would gladly watch the killer of that black kid drown in his own excrement, but he couldn't help respecting him for his foresight.

"It also means they went out deliberately that night to kill the yam—or somebody that looked like him."

"Maybe so."

"That also explains why Tommy's shitting in his pants. It was a Mob hit. Tommy's ass is on the line if he opens his mouth."

"Then, you'd better hope the Mafia did *not* have something to do with it. Tommy's your best hope."

"He'd have to be out of his mind to testify against the Mafia."

"The DA still has material I haven't seen yet. It might indicate whether or not there was a link to organized crime. If there was, we may have to rethink our strategy."

"What do you know about the guy who was killed?"

Ira shrugged as he sifted through some papers. "Youth worker for the Flatbush Civic Improvement Association. Twenty-three years old. No arrest record."

"That's it?"

"Unless the DA knows something. The kid looked clean—a social worker."

"That doesn't make sense. Why would a Mafia hit man go out of his way to kill a black social worker?"

But Ira seemed to have lost interest in the subject.

"I'll talk to McCready and be back in touch with you in a couple days."

"Look into the background of this Andrew Mott character."

"I'll do what I can. I have three other murder trials pending, and I've only got two hands." Ira offered his girlish palm and gave his client a brave smile. "See you soon."

Billy's first inclination after talking to his lawyer was to get in touch with his Mafioso visitor and accept whatever offer the Mob was willing to make. With Tommy McCready sitting on the fence, he had about as much chance of beating this charge as Rosemary Grady did of making sainthood.

But he felt an instinctive appetite for a good fight, especially one waged in a just cause—certainly a novelty in his short life. Mostly his career had been a series of intricate lies designed to beat somebody out of something—usually dope. The closest he had ever come to warring on the side of the angels was when he was questioned about a burglary he did not commit—a professional job well beyond the talents of someone like himself or Brendan. But he had been so scared he might actually be tagged with that caper, he hadn't had time to think about the glory he would amass fighting for his own innocence.

This time was different. Little Billy had turned this case into an entirely different matter, one being played out not just for his own skin but for something bigger and better than himself—a concept that had never been part of his lexicon before Rosemary presented him with the fruit of his loins. He wasn't even fond of the kid. What made the boy loom so large in his thinking was the idea of paternity itself. It was as if he had been called upon to act as pope or president or some other office of great responsibility which no ordinary person would dream of being called to.

Even so, he still had to choose between perhaps a hundred thousand dollars, which would go far toward securing his son's future, or fighting for his acquittal, with the possibility of doing several long years in prison if he lost. What would his own father have done in these circumstances? he wondered as he stared up at the damp ceiling over his bunk while his cellmate lay in the bunk below giggling.

The idea of his father finding himself the object of a criminal prosecution was absurd. William Conover, Sr. was an upstanding, church-going rock. He didn't even drink—at least not in the sense his son understood drinking. He held a steady job, brought home a paycheck intact every Friday and loved his wife and children. How could he, Billy, use a man like that as a model?

He continued to study all the law he could get his hands on. He learned a lot about procedure but not much to give him a leg up on the charge itself. Everything seemed to come down to who the jury believed—himself or Bruno's friends.

Toward the end of the week he heard again from the Mob. This time it was just a note passed to him by one of the guards who also did a sideline in acid. The note was written in a child's large, precise hand: "100."

Ira returned at the end of the week.

"One of the black kids is a possible. But you have to remember, he couldn't pick anybody out of a lineup."

"He had no trouble picking *me* out."

"You have blond hair."

"That makes me a murderer?"

"It makes you memorable to a black kid for whom a lot of white people look alike."

"For whom *white* people look alike?"

Ira removed his glasses and rubbed his eyes with his knuckles. With his glasses off he looked like a newborn kitten.

"Those kids were scared," he said. "They all ran off except for the youth worker. Even if this potential witness stopped to watch what was going on, any prosecutor worth his salt could punch all sorts of holes in his testimony. He had to be watching from fifty or sixty feet away."

"Where does all this leave me?"

Ira put his glasses on again.

"About six inches from where we were the last time we met."

"Which is sweet piss-all."

"We could go to trial with what we have and hope the black kid or your friend Tommy comes through..."

"Forget Tommy," Billy said. "His own ass is on the line."

"...or we can try to make a deal."

"What deal?"

Ira set his mouth as if anticipating an argument.

"Man Two."

"That's two-to-five years."

Ira nodded.

"And if we take it to trial?"

"You lose, you're looking at big time."

Two years for certain versus a possible twenty-five if he lost.

"But, Ira," he said, "I'm innocent!"

The lawyer regarded him as if he had been placed in this uncomfortable position all too often.

"It's your call, Billy. I'll take it any way you want."

He had faced choices in the past and been able to make a decision—when a cop had him dead-to-rights with stolen property in his pocket and he could stay or run; when he had the option of beating a dealer or another junkie out of some choice goods but had to risk the consequences. What made this morning's decision so difficult was the novelty of being innocent.

"No," he said with a finality which seemed to take the lawyer by surprise.

"No?"

Billy shook his head vigorously. He was angry now, but it was a clean, righteous feeling, not at all like the wild rages he usually felt. "I ain't copping no plea. Why should I? I didn't waste that kid."

"You're sure? You know the possible consequences."

"I'm sure. I'm about as fucking sure as I'm ever gonna be."

# CHAPTER TWENTY-ONE

Two weeks later the case came to trial.

Billy had seen his share of courtrooms, but those had all been in Criminal Court, cavernous halls where hundreds of people congregated and the judge barely cast a glance in the direction of the defendant before hurrying on to the next plea bargain. But this was a Class A felony and as such warranted the upscale ambience of Brooklyn Supreme. Here the courtrooms were of a modest size and for the most part empty, the benches undarkened by decades of cheap clothing rubbing daily against them. The walls were wood-paneled and well-maintained. And, most impressive of all, the place was quiet as a church.

He got only a brief glimpse of the spectators the case had attracted as he was escorted to his seat behind a large table on the defendant's side of the courtroom. He estimated twenty-five or thirty people were gathered for the proceedings—his mother and sister, a few friends from the block, some reporters, and the rest friends, he assumed, of other defendants or the deceased. He was looking for the fireplug who had offered him money to take a dive for Abruzzi when the court officer ordered everyone to rise. A middle-age black woman climbed up onto the bench. Billy turned toward his lawyer to protest but was brusquely hushed.

"You can't object to a judge's color," Ira whispered a few seconds later. "Besides, we could have done worse."

"Yeah, right. We could've got a black *man*."

The ADA made her opening statement. A fortyish woman even slighter than Ira, she tried to compensate for her lack of stature with three-inch heels. The effect was to make her look even smaller, and the effort required to keep herself upright on spikes seemed to require her constant attention. As she laid out her case Billy paid close attention to the jury. To a person, they seemed as preoccupied with her odd appearance as with her words.

"Finally, the prosecution will prove beyond the shadow of a reasonable doubt that William James Conover, Jr."—he felt an unpleasant thrill hearing his full name pronounced in public—"did knowingly and with malice aforethought murder Andrew Van Buren Mott in cold blood and should on that account receive the full measure of the law's justice."

Even though she was talking about his conviction for a crime that could cost him the rest of his life, he admired her high-flown rhetoric. He especially liked "the law's full measure," which reminded him of Shakespeare, an author he had much admired in a curriculum which contained very little else to admire.

Ira rose to speak. Compared with the prosecution he looked full-size now, but he had none of her gifts for public speaking. Instead of declaiming as she had done, he spoke in a low apologetic tone. Billy noted that some members of the jury, especially a couple old women in the back row, were straining to hear. At one point the judge asked the young lawyer to please speak up. As if roused from some personal rumination, Ira glanced up in surprise, then went on in the same inaudible drone.

When he sat down again at the defense table there were thick beads of sweat on his brow.

The prosecution called its first witness, Joseph Vitale, the young man Billy had sat next to the night of the murder and one of the two who had exited the car with him in Prospect Park.

In the light of day Vitale looked older than his twenty years. He had on a conservative double-breasted suit that made him look a little like a Wall Street wunderkind. Billy wondered whether the tailoring had been the prosecution's idea or the Mob's, as he fingered the lapel of his own royal blue suit which he knew made his eyes even more appealing.

Vitale gave his occupation as part-time construction worker.

"When did you first meet the defendant William Conover, Mr. Vitale?" the ADA asked, treading a small circle in front of the raised witness box like a Chihuahua walking on its hind legs.

"I only met him that night. The night he wasted the black kid."

Ira objected, his eagerness taking Billy by surprise after such a lackluster opening statement. The judge sustained him.

"You never laid eyes on him before?" the prosecution continued.

"No."

"Then, Mr. Vitale, you had no reason to...hold any kind of grudge against the defendant?"

"I'm sorry?" he said, leaning forward like someone hard of hearing.

"You had no reason to be out to 'get' the defendant?"

The witness seemed to consider this question carefully. Then he shook his head definitively.

"No, ma'am. I didn't know him from Adam."

The ADA went on to lay out step by step what happened that night—the ride out Ocean Parkway, the turn onto Flatbush Avenue, the exiting of the car—all more or less the way it happened. Then she asked the witness to describe "in his own words" what happened next, and turned away from the witness box as if to show there were no strings attached to him from any part of her person. Indeed, it was as if she had no more interest now in what he was going to say than if she were a spectator herself who had wandered into the courtroom by chance.

"He got out of the car. Then he walked up to the black kid...Mott," he added, hesitating on the name. "Then he raised the gun to the black kid's head and said something. Then the black kid said something back. The next thing I know, the gun goes off."

"He fired the weapon at Mr. Mott," the ADA said, taking an interest again.

"Yeah, that's right."

"You saw him fire the weapon, at close range."

"Yes, ma'am."

"Do you see the person who fired the gun sitting in this courtroom?"

"Yeah, sure."

"Would you please point him out for us?"

He pointed at Billy, although Billy had a strong sense that this was the first time the young man had ever really looked at him and that if he hadn't been sitting in the defendant's chair, Vitale would have pointed at whoever was in fact occupying it.

"Let the record show the witness has identified the defendant, William Conover."

Ira got up to cross-examine. He took two or three quick steps toward the witness box as if hot to get on with it, then suddenly came to a halt. He remained standing a good six feet from the witness who, following the ADA's questioning, was looking rather pleased with himself, as if he had just answered a difficult catechism quiz or cleanly broken the legs of a loan deadbeat.

"Mr. Vitale," Ira began in a high voice, "you have testified that the car you and the defendant were riding in that night turned off Ocean Parkway and onto Flatbush Avenue. Correct?"

"Yeah."

"Whose idea was that?"

The witness frowned. "Whose idea?"

"Who was it that said to turn onto Flatbush?"

Vitale glanced toward the court spectators.

"His, I guess."

"By 'his' you mean whom?"

Vitale pointed toward the defense table again.

"You are pointing at the defendant?"

The witness nodded. The judge made him confirm his nod with a spoken response.

Ira made one of those little pirouettes Billy had seen the prosecutor execute when she seemed confident of what the witness was going to say next.

"How did he communicate that decision to the driver?"

"I'm sorry?"

"What did he say to the driver of the vehicle to indicate that he, Billy, wanted him to turn onto Flatbush Avenue?"

Vitale shrugged. "I dunno. 'Turn here,' I guess."

"You're not sure?"

"No."

"Maybe it was someone else who told the driver to turn. Maybe nobody told the driver to turn."

Vitale seemed to give this possibility more thought than in his opinion it deserved, then said, "Naw, Billy told him. I don't remember his exact words, but he told him."

Ira then asked about the moments just before they drove down Billy's block.

"Whose idea was it to pick up the defendant?"

"Nobody's."

"He just turned up?"

"Sort off."

"Nobody in the car said, 'We have to stop to pick up somebody'?"

"I don't think so."

"So, Billy just came along for the ride, so to speak."

The prosecution objected, saying the question was vague and misleading. The judge upheld the objection and ordered the witness to answer only what he knew from his own personal experience.

"Did you, Joseph Vitale, ever hear anyone in the car say anything about picking up a fifth passenger prior to the time Thomas McCready actually stopped to ask Billy if he wanted to come along?"

"No."

"Thank you, Mr. Vitale. Your Honor, I have no more questions at this time."

The other passenger that night in the back seat with Billy was called to the stand.

This time the prosecutor skipped the matter of whether Billy asked to have the car driven to Flatbush Avenue. She concentrated on the shooting itself. After the same "in your own words" prompting, the witness testified he saw Billy pull the trigger and kill Andrew Mott.

"Then what happened?"

A younger, less athletic version of Vitale, he shrugged just as his predecessor had done before answering.

"We all got in the car and drove off."

"You drove in what direction?"

"Up Flatbush Avenue."

"That would be north?"

"Toward the park."

"Toward Prospect Park. Did the car actually enter the park?"

"Yeah, on that highway in there."

"The car entered the circular park drive. You drove past the lake?"

"Yeah."

"Then what happened?"

"We stopped."

"Who asked that the car be stopped?"

The witness jerked his head toward the defendant's table.

"The defendant asked that Tommy McCready stop the car?"

"Right."

"Do you remember the words he used?"

"He said, 'Pull over here. This is where I get out'—something like that."

"There's no doubt in your mind that it was Mr. Conover who asked the driver to stop the car?"

"Uh uh."

The ADA paused as if plunged into introspection. Then she did a slow half-turn.

"Did the defendant take anything with him when he exited the car?"

"Yeah."

"What did he take with him?"

"The piece."

"By which you mean the gun which killed Andrew Mott?"

"Right."

She walked over to a table next to the court stenographer, a young woman who seemed to be paying the same distracted attention to what was going on as Billy's mother did to TV soap operas while she was ironing. The ADA picked up something heavy in a large plastic bag and carried it to the witness stand, holding it well away from her person. With some difficulty, she handed it up to the witness.

"Is this the gun Mr. Conover took with him when he exited the car in Prospect Park?"

The witness regarded the object in the plastic bag with admiration.

"That's it."

The prosecutor formerly introduced the weapon into evidence and returned it to the exhibit table.

"Mr. D'Elleto, did you accompany the defendant after he exited the car?"

"We got out the same time."

"Was he carrying the gun?"

"Yes."

"What happened then?"

"We split up."

"You went separate ways."

"Right."

"And to the best of your knowledge, when you split up the defendant was still in possession of the murder weapon."

"He still had it."

"Thank you. No more questions, Your Honor."

Ira asked the witness if anyone had asked Billy to take the gun with him when he left the car, but D'Elleto replied he didn't remember anything like that.

"No one else in the car handed him the gun and asked him to get rid of it in the Park?"

"Uh uh."

"Mr. D'Elleto, where were you sitting in the car before it stopped in Prospect Park?"

"In the back."

"Alongside Billy Conover."

"Against the other door."

"Joseph Vitale was sitting between you and Billy, is that right?"

"Yeah."

"Who handed the weapon to Billy? Joseph? Or was it someone in the front?"

The witness leaned forward before answering. "Handed it?"

"Your Honor," the prosecution interrupted, "the defense is trying to lead the witness."

The judge agreed with a stern look at the young Legal Aid attorney.

"Who," Ira went on, "was actually holding the gun during the ride back from Flatbush—after the killing, that is?"

The witness shrugged. "Billy, I guess."

"You 'guess'? You're not sure?"

"Yeah, I'm sure. Billy had it."

"You saw it in his hands?"

The witness laughed self-consciously.

"Hey, it was dark in that backseat."

"So the defendant may or may not actually have been in possession of the murder weapon during the ride away from the scene of the crime."

167

"Naw, I didn't say that."

"Well, then," Ira said, taking a firm step toward him, "what exactly *do* you say?"

D'Elleto glanced toward the prosecution side of the courtroom.

"Like I said, he had the gun when he got out of the car. That's all I know."

"That's all you know? You don't know if the weapon was put into his hands by someone else?"

The witness swallowed hard and shook his head from side to side, avoiding eye contact with the defense attorney.

"He had the gun when we got out of the car."

Ira paused for a couple seconds, then turned abruptly away.

"No more questions."


"That went better than I expected," Ira told Billy during the trial's first recess.

"It did?"

"Just a little chink in their armor. But reasonable doubt is something you insinuate into the minds of a jury by degrees."

Billy caught the lawyer's general drift. And any sign of optimism was good, even from a second-rate Legal Aid.

"I never touched that gun till Tommy handed it to me."

"Which explains why his prints were on it as well as your own."

"Exactly."

The two sat quietly, each wrapped in his own thoughts. Billy could hear muted conversation behind him. He turned and saw his mother was no longer sitting next to his sister. He made an inquiring gesture, and Cathleen mouthed the words "Ladies Room," causing them both to smile. Then he himself mouthed, "How are you?"

She replied with a wink.

The prosecution called one of the teenagers who had been standing on the street corner where Andrew Mott was killed. Lanky and big-eyed, he looked even younger than his seventeen years and seemed extremely nervous. The ADA brought her best box-side manner to bear, but her clumsy efforts to step out of her hard-nose persona only caused the young man to react with more apprehension.

"Were you present at the time the red car pulled up to the corner where Andrew Mott was standing?"

"Yes, I was."

Then she began her "in your own words" question and took the obligatory three steps away from the witness box as if he were now on automatic pilot. But as nervous as she had made him when she was standing directly in front of the witness box, when he saw her desert him entirely the young man froze up with anxiety.

After a few seconds of silence, the prosecutor realized something was amiss and turned back toward her witness.

"Go ahead, Mr. Gates."

But he seemed incapable of speech. It was only when the judge, a more familiar figure, if not in this particular role, leaned over the bench and said, "You go ahead, son, and tell us what you saw," that he found his tongue again.

"I seen him shoot Mr. Mott."

"You saw *who* shoot Andrew Mott?" the ADA prompted.

The witness hesitantly pointed a long finger toward the table where Billy was seated.

"That boy over there."

"The witness is indicating the defendant," the ADA said. "Your witness."

Ira half-stood up and said, "I have no questions of the witness at this time, your Honor. But I reserve the right to recall him later."

The judge raised her eyebrows as if to say, "It's your funeral," then brought her gavel down decisively and announced a lunch break.

Billy sat out lunch in a holding cell. For company, he had a defendant also accused of murder—his wife and two children—and an assortment of car thieves, drug dealers and stickup men.

He had no appetite for the ham-and-swiss box lunch. He sipped a cup of weak, tepid coffee.

When he returned to court and was waiting for the proceeding to get under way, he was struck by the casual manner of the court employees. The officers chatted and laughed, picking the remains of their own more palatable meals from their teeth. The prosecutor was engaged in an amiable conversation that seemed to have nothing to do with the prospect of sending him to jail for the next quarter century. Even his own lawyer, when he finally appeared just a couple minutes before the judge was due back on the stand, seemed preoccupied with other matters, probably a last-minute call to remind his wife that he had a bowling date that evening.

"How was lunch?" Billy asked in a sarcastic tone as Ira hastily unpacked his briefcase.

"What lunch? I spent the last hour trying to sort out my notes."

He pulled a mangled manila folder out of his case and removed from it a stack of yellow sheets covered with small, cramped handwriting. "And yours?"

"Fine," Billy said. "Just fine."

The prosecution's next witness was Tommy McCready. Tommy gave his employment as mason's apprentice. That was news to Billy.

"Mr. McCready, you were driving the car that night, were you not?"

"Yes, I was," Tommy said, looking dapper in a new blue suit that reminded Billy of the school uniforms they used to wear in Holy Family. Only, in those days the tie also would have been blue instead of red-and-black stripe.

"Whose idea was it to drive to Flatbush?"

Tommy glanced toward Billy.

"His," he replied with a jerk of his head.

"By 'his,' do you mean the defendant, Billy Conover?"

"Yes, ma'am."

"Thank you. No more questions of this witness, Your Honor."

Ira seemed so preoccupied with his notes that Billy thought he didn't realize the prosecution had finished. But then the lawyer slowly got to his feet, still studying the yellow sheets in his hand like a student trying to get the last possible advantage before taking a difficult exam.

He walked deliberately toward the witness box. Tommy watched with no sign of the previous witness's nerves. Billy himself felt a curious lack of resentment at the lie his old schoolmate had just told. He knew Tommy was only trying to save his own skin. There was no telling what kind of "offer" the Mob had made if he didn't cooperate.

"Mr. McCready, you have testified that it was the defendant who asked that you drive to Flatbush. Is that correct?"

"Yes."

"Where were you intending to drive there before you picked him up?"

"I beg your pardon?"

"Before you saw him walking down 16th Street that night. There were four of you in the car up to that point, if I'm not mistaken. Is that right?"

"Yes."

"Where were you headed before you spotted Billy?"

Tommy hesitated, shrugged and said, "We wasn't headed no place."

"You were just...out for a ride?"

"Yeah."

Ira took a little stroll around the area in front of the witness box.

"Whose idea was it to go for a ride in the first place?"

"Whose idea?"

"Yes."

"I guess it was mine.... Or maybe one of the other guys'."

"These other guys, are they all friends of yours?"

Tommy colored a bit but said, "Sure, they're friends."

"Good friends?"

"Pretty good friends."

"For how long have you been friends with, say, Mr. D'Elleto?"

Tommy shrugged. "A couple months."

"And Mr. Vitale?"

"I dunno. About the same."

"How about Bruno Abruzzi?"

Tommy's expression changed. His eyes dropped and his pink flush became deeper.

"I only met him that night."

Ira turned directly toward the witness as if he had just heard something that surprised him.

"You only met him that evening?"

"Right."

"Why was that?"

"He was...is...a friend of Joey's. He just came along for the ride."

"Where did you pick him up?"

"Down around 65th Street."

"65th Street in Brooklyn?"

"Right."

"You live on 21st Street, don't you, Mr. McCready?"

"Yes."

But you went all the way down to 65th Street to pick up someone you've just told us you would only be meeting for the first time. Why was that?"

"'Cause that's what Joey wanted to do."

"Joseph D'Elleto."

"Right."

"Mr. McCready, when did you decide to go for this ride?"

"That night."

"How soon before you picked up Billy Conover?"

Tommy cocked his head to one side and thought for a moment.

"I dunno. Half an hour."

"And how did you come to take Mr. D'Elleto and Mr. Vitale along? Never mind about Mr. Abruzzi for the moment."

Tommy squared his jaw, looked the young lawyer in the eye but flushed as he replied, "They was hanging in the neighborhood."

"Whose neighborhood?"

"Mine."

"Mr. McCready, are you aware where both of those young men live?"

"Yeah, Mill Basin."

"Is that neighborhood anywhere near 21st Street?"

Tommy snickered. "Naw. It's about four five miles away."

"So how is it they turned up suddenly in your neighborhood just at the time you decided to go for a ride?"

Tommy shrugged. "I dunno."

Ira stood in front of the box and stared at the witness. Tommy's brow furrowed, relaxed, then furrowed again. For the first couple seconds he tried to maintain eye contact with the lawyer, then he looked away.

Finally the judge said, "Mr. Greenberg, do you have any more questions of this witness?"

"Not at this time, Your Honor."

# CHAPTER TWENTY-TWO

The prosecution rested its case and the judge called a halt to the proceedings for the day.

"You gonna call Abruzzi in the morning?"

"First thing," Ira said, packing up his case and looking a good deal more positive than Billy thought he had a right to. But then, it was he, not the lawyer, who was on trial.

"You got some secret plan how to get him to confess?"

"Not quite. But we haven't shot our last arrow yet. Try to get a good night's sleep."

"Sure," Billy said as the court officers began to cuff him. "No problem."

It stormed all night. The thunder even penetrated the thick walls of the House of Detention. The storm reminded Billy of the storms of his youth when he and his friends ran from tree to tree in Prospect Park playing rain tag. What they were really playing tag with was the lightning, though none of them realized how dangerous the game was. Danger still gave him a rush, and what was there to live for if not the rushes life provided? Even lying on a hard bunk waiting for this long night to pass, he still got a thrill from each loud thunderclap and hoped for more, louder ones.

Not so his cellmate. Throughout the storm, the man cowered in his bunk with his pillow over his head. Billy tried to engage him in conversation, but the most he got in reply was a muffled grunt. Finally, near midnight, the thunder became more distant, the lightning moderated and the accused pornographer emerged from beneath his pillow.

"You always freak when it thunders and lightnings?" Billy said, feeling as exhilarated as if he had swallowed a couple ups.

"Ever since I was a kid."

"What'd you do if you was out on a date or driving on the highway or something?"

"I didn't go out on many dates."

"You're into all that sex and you didn't go out with girls?"

"I didn't need to go out on dates to get sex."

Billy thought this over for a moment in the light of his own experience. The last time he had gone out on a date was a sophomore dance in high school. He tried to put his hand inside the girl's panties when they were dancing a slow number in a dark corner of the gymnasium. One of the brothers caught him at it. "Come to think of it, I ain't gone out on many dates myself, and I guess I make out pretty good."

"It's all in knowing how to get around them."

"Right," Billy said. "Like saying what they want to hear. How beautiful they are, shit like that."

"Exactly," his cellmate replied, his voice sounding more like the confident expert. "Like the time I got this girl to blow me in a movie theater."

"Back in Ohio?"

"Right. Then afterwards she blew me again in the parking lot. Then she let me take pictures of her."

"Like the ones they said they caught you with in your apartment?"

"Naw, not shit like that. Artistic poses. You know, like with her sitting on the kitchen table butt-naked with a rolling pin between her legs. Or smearing herself all over with Karo syrup. That was the best one, because I got to lick it off."

"Sounds wild."

"That was just kid stuff," he went on, his voice deep now and full of itself. "I could tell you stuff you wouldn't believe."

"Try me."

The man laughed. "You ain't old enough. Besides, you might go and tell the DA."

"Are you nuts?"

"Hey," the man replied in a menacing tone so much like a Hollywood psycho that Billy had to stifle a laugh, "don't ever say that."

"Okay, okay. So, tell me what else you did."

They passed the next hours trading sex stories—rather, his cellmate told sex stories and Billy countered with tales of derring-do, like the time he crossed the Kosciusko Bridge jumping from girder to girder of the substructure with nothing beneath him but a hundred feet of polluted air.

When they had exhausted their stock of tales Billy suggested they catch some shuteye.

"Wait. I want to tell you one more," his cellmate said in a voice that reached Billy through a haze of fatigue and memories of other stories about nymphomaniacs and telescopes trained on nunneries full of sexual deviants. "One time me and my pal got this retard girl to come down into a cellar with us. She was the village idiot, you know? She didn't live nowhere. So we figured nobody'd miss her for a couple days at least."

"Uh huh," Billy said, half asleep. He had himself embellished considerably on the stories he told and took it for granted his cellmate was doing the same.

"First we got her to take off all her clothes. Then we told her to get inside the old furnace—it was summertime, so the fire was out."

Billy was already dreaming about a stretch of beach like the one at the Rockaways where his father took the family when he was a kid. The sand was bright with sunlight, the water was green and the sky like a brilliant blue bowl. But suddenly the image of a retarded girl who used to live on 16th Street appeared in his dream. His friends used to invite her into various cellars and get her to jerk them off. Even though he had sex with most of the young willing women in that neighborhood, including a few of the married ones, something made him balk about having anything to do with that retarded girl. He saw her clearly now in his almost-dream—getting stuffed into a furnace.

"At first we were just gonna scare her—you know, lock her up for a couple minutes till she screamed and begged to come out. But then we kind of liked it with her in there. We figured, hell, nobody'd miss her anyway. She was just a retard. She didn't live no place in particular. So we decided to leave her there."

There was silence for the next several moments. Then Billy asked as casually as he could, his limbs trembling unaccountably, "So what happened?"

He heard a chuckle from the bunk below.

"Somebody found her a couple days later. They took her away someplace. We never seen her again."

"Took her away where?"

"I dunno. One of them institutions, I guess. Which was where she belonged. She was the stupidest fucking cunt I ever was with."

The next morning Ira looked agitated. After dumping most of his satchel onto the defense table, he plunged into some notes, put them down, picked up other notes, read for a few seconds, then put them down as well. Finally he took off his glasses and began rubbing his forehead.

"Something wrong?" Billy said, feeling like someone who was watching a prizefighter he has bet his last nickel on complain about double vision. "Fucking Rules of Procedure," the lawyer answered as if Billy were a legal acquaintance instead of his client. "I prepare a case with one set of premises, then the DA informs me that Discovery does not include half the information he has in his possession."

Billy was familiar now with terms like Rules of Procedure and Discovery, but he didn't have a clue to what Ira was talking about.

"What it boils down to," the attorney said, regarding Billy with that glassless new-born-kitten look, "is the judge has ruled that any information about the witness's past record and associations that don't pertain directly to this case will be inadmissible."

"That's bad?"

"That's very bad. It's also illegal. But if a defendant can't afford to pay for an appeal, what difference does it make if the judge decides to make up her own rules as she goes along? She may as well invoke the Writs of Assistance, for Christ's sake. Nobody'd give a damn if the case can't be taken to Appeals."

He took a second dive into his notes as if resigned to his fate— although the only fate that mattered here, as far as Billy could see, was his own. This wasn't the kind of upbeat note he had hoped to start out on this, the most critical day of his trial.

"The Defense calls Bruno Abruzzi," Ira declared after the court was called to order.

The killer himself, dressed in a subdued blue suit which made him look like the most respectable person in the courtroom, sauntered slowly toward the witness box and was administered the oath. Ira asked him his address and employment. Then he said, "Mr. Abruzzi, did you accompany Thomas McCready for an automobile ride on the night of March 28th of this year?"

"Yes, I did," Abruzzi replied in a gravelly voice, his eye all but healed, Billy noted.

"And was the defendant Billy Conover in the same car for part of that ride?"

"Yes."

Ira took one of his little walks away from the witness box, a sure sign that a critical question was upcoming.

"Please tell us, Mr. Abruzzi, what happened after you reached Flatbush that night," then added as if unable to resist, "in your own words."

The witness shrugged and shifted about on his seat.

"Billy over there, he wasted the Negro guy."

Ira turned back toward the witness box.

"You saw this happen?"

"Correct."

"Where exactly did you see it from. Inside the car? Outside?"

Abruzzi hesitated a second. "Inside, I guess."

"You don't remember?"

"Inside. Yeah, inside the car."

"Mr. Abruzzi," Ira said, going off on another jaunt, "let me get this straight. You're telling the court that after the car stopped on Flatbush Avenue and all the other people in it got out, you yourself chose to remain inside. Is that right?"

The witness regarded Ira silently for a moment, then cast a glance toward the ADA before affirming that, yes, that was the case.

"Is there any particular reason why you decided not to get out of the car with the others?"

Abruzzi crossed his hands on his lap and seemed to relax as if all the hard questions were over.

"I didn't want to get involved."

"You didn't want to get involved? Are you aware, Mr. Abruzzi, that two of the people who were in the car that night have sworn in their depositions that everyone got out of the car, including yourself?"

"Well, they were wrong."

"You did not get out of the car?"

"Correct."

Ira took another stroll, then asked, "Do you happen to know what kind of gun was used in the shooting?"

The prosecution objected.

"Your Honor," Ira continued, "I'm trying to establish just how much of what went on that night Mr. Abruzzi was aware of. The murder weapon and who had possession of it at different points of the evening is essential information."

The judge overruled the objection.

"Please answer the question, Mr. Abruzzi."

"It was a nine mil."

"By which you mean a nine millimeter automatic?"

"Exactly."

"Is that a gun you're personally familiar with?"

Again the prosecution objected. This time the judge sustained.

"Let me put it to you this way, Mr. Abruzzi. Have you ever seen a nine millimeter automatic?"

"Yes."

"Have you ever held one in your hand?"

"Yes."

"Under what circumstances?"

"I used to go to a range."

"A firing range?"

"Correct."

"To shoot?"

"With my friend. He has a permit."

"For a nine millimeter automatic?"

"Correct."

"Did you ever fire the weapon yourself?"

"Like I said, my friend had the permit. I couldn't fire no weapon without a permit."

"But you gained a pretty good knowledge of how one works."

"You could say that."

"Thank you. No more questions at this time, your Honor."


"Are you fucking crazy?" Billy asked when Ira sat down. "Aren't you gonna tell him you know he did the killing?"

"I'm not a witness, Billy. The judge wouldn't allow it."

"What d'ya mean? He's the killer, ain't he?"

"But he's not on trial. I'm here to defend *you*, not prosecute somebody else, even if they're guilty as sin."

Billy had never heard anybody but his mother use that expression. It seemed odd coming from a Jewish lawyer.

"At this time, Your Honor, the defense would like to recall Thomas McCready to the stand."

McCready came forward, was told he was still under oath and sat down. He looked even more nervous than he did the first time.

"Mr. McCready, how long have you known the defendant?"

Tommy brightened a bit. "Billy? I know him, jeez, fifteen years?"

"You went to elementary school together, is that right?"

"Right. Holy Family."

"And you've kept in touch ever since?"

"We see each other around the neighborhood."

"Would you call Billy a friend?"

Tommy thought for a moment, happy to have something both truthful and positive to say, then moved his shoulders and head up and down in unison.

"Yeah, sure."

Ira turned toward the jury box where three black women in the front row were sitting up very straight, and said, "Did you consider him a friend the night you picked him up on 16th Street?"

Again Tommy bobbed his head in the affirmative. "Sure."

"A friend you wouldn't want to do any harm to?"

The prosecution objected.

"Your Honor," Ira explained, "I'm trying to determine the nature of the relationship between this witness and my client for the sake of establishing testimonial credibility."

Billy had the feeling his lawyer could have answered the objection less legalistically but preferred to speak in a code Tommy would not easily understand. His estimation of the man went up a notch.

The judge overruled the objection and instructed the witness to answer.

"Naw, I wouldn't wanna to do Billy no harm," Tommy said, dropping his eyes.

Ira took a step closer.

"You understand your testimony is crucial in this case, don't you, Mr. McCready?"

Again the prosecution objected. This time the judge sustained it.

"Mr. McCready," Ira said, "if Billy Conover did not fire the murder weapon that night, he is innocent. I'm sure you understand that."

Tommy said nothing. The ADA was on her feet nonetheless, but held off with her objection.

"You also understand that you are under oath and would be committing perjury if you did not tell the truth about what you know."

The judge asked the defense to explain where he was heading.

"Your Honor, Tommy McCready was in a position to know exactly what happened on that street corner in Flatbush. I'm merely trying to impress upon him the importance of his testimony."

"That's all well and good, Counsel, but suppose you leave the instruction to me and get on with your questioning."

Ira turned back toward the witness box.

"Mr. McCready, did you with your own eyes see Billy Conover fire that gun and kill the deceased, Andrew Mott?"

Tommy stared back at the attorney red-faced, then glanced toward Billy like a little kid who had just done something in his pants. He dropped his eyes.

"I heard the shot. Then I saw the y—... I saw the black guy fall to the ground."

"Mr. McCready, I'll ask you again: Did you see Billy Conover fire the weapon that killed Andrew Mott?"

Tommy continued to stare down at his lap but said nothing.

"Answer the question," the judge said.

Tommy looked up at her as if realizing for the first time there was anyone else in the courtroom besides himself and the defense attorney. Then he fixed his eyes on the back wall of the courtroom.

"Yes."

"I remind you that you are under oath," Ira snapped. "Perjury is a felony, Mr. McCready. I'll ask you one more time: Did you see Billy kill Mr. Mott? Or did you see someone else do it, someone who's sitting in this courtroom right now?"

At the last question Tommy seemed to snap out of his funk. His eyes darted toward the benches where the friends and relations of Bruno Abruzzi were sitting. Then they glazed over.

"That's right," he said in a flat voice. "I seen Billy do it."

"Damn!" Ira said after the judge had called a five-minute recess. "I had him by the balls and let him slip away."

Billy wasn't sure what he was referring to but said, "Hey, you did the best you could. The guy's shitting a brick what happens to him if he comes clean. I'd probably do the same thing in his spot."

But Ira didn't seem to be listening.

# CHAPTER TWENTY-THREE

Billy was the next and last scheduled witness. But it was already late in the day when Ira finished his questioning, so he asked for a recess until the following morning. He and Billy had already gone over his own testimony at length, so there was little left to do but wait until his own turn came to take the stand.

"Get a good night's sleep," Ira suggested as if his client were not going back to a hard smelly cot in a cell inhabited by a homicidal sex pervert.

Ever since he had decided to take the case to trial, Billy had been imagining how he would give his own testimony. Usually he pictured his time on the stand as a showdown where truth was vindicated, justice done and evil overcome. He could not imagine any jury taking a sleaze like Abruzzi's word over his own sincere assertions. But as he had watched the trial unfold he had come to see that justice was not always served up according to script, at least not the script in his mind, which was heavily influenced by Hollywood movies and various TV legal dramas. He was coming to understand his fate hung by a thread. If it were he sitting on the jury instead of three heavy black women and an assortment of retirees, clerks and secretaries, he would be hard-pressed to decide whether or not there was reasonable doubt about his guilt.

Half an hour after lights-out he was beginning to wonder if he would get any sleep at all when he heard the approaching steps of a guard. He assumed the screw was coming for his cellmate and even imagined they were about to fry him in the electric chair for his sordid crimes, and deservedly so.

"Counsel visit," the officer announced.

"My lawyer?" Billy said as the man locked the cell behind him. "At this hour?"

The guard gave him a nudge toward the door which led to the elevator to the visitation room. During the ride down Billy racked his mind to figure out what could have gotten Ira out of bed at midnight. Had he come up with new evidence? Was the case suddenly dead in the water because of some unhappy development? Or had one of the attorney's relations suddenly died and he had come to announce that somebody else was taking over the case?

He suspected the last as the most likely possibility and entered the visiting area with a sinking feeling.

"Hello, Billy," Ira said, for once not rummaging in his battered briefcase. He was also out of uniform, having replaced his worn suit with a pair of jeans and a plaid sport shirt.

"What's up?"

Ira joined his hands on the empty table between them and said, "A deal."

"Deal? What kind of deal?"

The DA's offering Man One. I got a call half an hour ago."

Billy was tempted to ask how much hard cash went with it but settled for a sardonic bark at the irony of the DA's offering him the same fate, for no recompense, that the Mob had offered for $100,000.

"I made a joke?" Ira said, looking put out by his client's amusement.

"Don't mind me, I'm just a little whacked out."

"Well, what do you say? A certain five-to-seven versus a possible twenty-five-to-life."

Billy took a deep breath and asked, "What, may I ask, has induced the DA to such generosity?"

Ira shrugged.

"Who knows? Maybe she figures between Tommy McCready's hesitations and Abruzzi's criminal eyes the jury might see reasonable doubt."

"Just what I was beginning to think myself."

"On the other hand, maybe she smells a hung jury. That would mean she has to repeat the entire process all over again at the taxpayer's expense. Personally, I look upon her offer as a win for you."

"You mean a win for *you*. I go to the slammer."

"But only for five, maybe even three years, instead of twenty-five. Plus, they'll drop the secondary charge of Reckless Endangerment."

"Hey, I if wanted to do time I would have accepted their offer the first time they made it."

Ira seemed disappointed. But Billy had already decided any choices he made in this matter now concerned someone other than himself. He had grown up fatherless because his own father had abandoned him—died, in point of fact, though for Billy it amounted to the same thing, even though the nuns and priests told him God had called his father to Him. Why should his own son care whether he was growing up fatherless because the man had willfully abandoned him or because the state had "called" him? The boy would become resentful and unforgiving, just as he, Billy, had. But, he decided, if he had to go to jail it was better for the boy that he at least do so proclaiming his innocence.

"Sorry, Ira. I appreciate the trouble you went to. But it's no deal. I didn't kill that kid, and I'm not gonna say I did."

"You don't actually have to admit to anything, Billy. You just plead guilty to a lesser charge. There's a difference."

"Not to me there ain't."

Ira leaned across the table.

"Billy, you're looking at serious time."

"I know that."

"With no possibility of parole until you're almost fifty. Think about it, Billy. That's most of your life—all your best years."

"Hey, who are you working for, me or the DA?"

"I'm trying to get you the best deal under the circumstances."

"You said yourself the prosecution must be unsure of their case, otherwise they wouldn't be offering no plea bargain."

"That's the likely explanation. But nobody can tell which way a jury will go."

"If we lose, I'll appeal."

"Appeals cost money. And on what grounds?"

"On the grounds that I fucking didn't do it!" he shouted, causing the guard who was keeping an eye on this conversation to take a step closer.

"Get real, Billy. Innocence has nothing to do with it. The only

184

question will be who the jury believes. The prosecution has three witnesses who say you pulled the trigger. The one witness we hoped would help clear you—that black kid who saw the shooting—makes a positive ID under oath."

"You haven't put *me* on the stand yet."

"That's right. But we can't be sure how that will work. What happens if the jury doesn't like the particular life style you've been were leading? What if the prosecution convinces them you're not the upstanding citizen we both know you to be?"

"Are you tryna be sarcastic?"

"I'm trying to be realistic. This whole trial hinges on who the jury believes."

"But you saw how Tommy looked on the stand. I wouldn't believe him if I was just asking for the time of day."

"That's how *you* saw him. You don't know what the jury saw."

"The prosecution must have seen the same thing. Otherwise, she wouldn't be getting cold feet."

"The prosecution wants a conviction. She'll take Man One if that's her best bet."

But Billy shook his head determinedly.

"I went this far. I go the whole way."


"Mr. Conover," Ira began the next morning, "how did you come to be in the car Tommy McCready was driving the night Andrew Mott was shot to death?"

Billy told him, and the attorney went on to elicit the events Billy had been party to after being picked up on 16th Street. He described them in a straightforward manner without comment, just as the lawyer had told him to do. As he spoke he began to have the feeling his truth-saying would cut through all the lies previously told and convince the jury of his innocence. Why should they not be convinced? Unlike the others, he was holding his head high and speaking in a firm, clear voice—not to mention the fine figure he cut in his one good suit. He was strangely free of nerves. All his life he had dissembled, sometimes merely out of habit. Being able to speak the truth in his own defense was a heady, liberating feeling.

"After you saw Mr. Abruzzi fire the murder weapon and return to the car, what happened then?"

"We drove away—fast."

"Mr. McCready drove away," Ira said, taking a stroll from the witness box the way Billy had seen him do with other witnesses. "And which direction did the car take?"

"Toward Prospect Park."

"Did it enter the park?"

"Yes."

"What happened next?"

Billy related how he was handed the gun by Tommy, his trek up the back of Monument Hill, his burying the weapon at the base of the fallen tree.

"What became of the other two people who exited the car at the same time you did?"

"They disappeared."

"What do you mean?"

"We split up."

"After you buried the gun, what did you do?"

"I headed down Monument Hill. But I spent the rest of the night in the park."

"Why was that?"

"I was afraid the cops might be looking for me—for all of us."

"When did you return home?"

"Sometime in the morning."

"I have no more questions, Your Honor."

The judge raised the sleeve of her long robe and peered down at her wrist. Then she turned toward the prosecution and said, "There'll be a five-minute recess."

"How'd I do?" Billy asked as they sat waiting for the proceedings to resume.

"Fine. Just do the same when the prosecution questions you."

Billy turned to see who was in the courtroom. Rosemary was sitting in the bench alongside Cathleen. Just behind them was his old friend Charlie Madigan. There was still no sign of Brendan.

"Mr. Conover," the ADA began when the judge returned, "you testified that you never touched the murder weapon until Tommy McCready handed it to you to dispose of in Prospect Park. Is that correct?"

"Yes, it is."

186

"And you say that you volunteered to bury the gun."

"I didn't exactly 'volunteer.' It was handed to me."

"But you agreed to dispose of it."

"I took it, yes."

"Why did you do that, Mr. Conover?" she asked, doing one of her slow pirouettes. Billy wondered if she was married, and if so, what there was of her to latch onto in bed, she seemed so insubstantial beneath her dark suit.

"Why did I do what?" he replied, having lost his train of thought.

"Why did you agree to dispose of the murder weapon if you had nothing to do with the killing?"

"Tommy's a friend."

"You did it for friendship?"

"I guess."

"You voluntarily put your own fingerprints on the murder weapon and then took on the burden of burying this same weapon—out of friendship?"

"Yes."

"Mr. Conover, just how much of a friend is Tommy McCready?"

"We know each other since grammar school."

"Would you say you were good friends?"

"Pretty good."

"You hang out together regularly?"

"Not so much anymore."

"Once a week? Twice a week?"

"Less."

"When, actually, was the last time you and Mr. McCready 'hung out' together?"

Billy felt himself blush and knew that wasn't good but tried to keep a confident tone in his voice.

"Maybe two, three weeks."

"Mr. Conover," she said, leaning close enough to the witness box that Billy could see where her mascara had been misapplied, "you and Tommy McCready haven't associated on a regular basis in almost five years. Isn't that so?"

"Time flies."

"So you accepted the murder weapon from a 'friend' who actually hasn't been a friend for some time, and agreed to dispose of it for him.

Is that what you expect us to believe, Mr. Conover? You risked going to prison for life just for the sake of old friendship?"

"Like I said, I wasn't thinking about it real hard. I just reacted."

"You just reacted. But you did have the presence of mind to send the other two young men away and then to carefully select a place to bury this weapon which you say you had never touched until Tommy McCready, your friend, asked you to dispose of it for him. And then you hid out in the park until you thought it was safe to return home."

His earlier vision of the truth cutting through the fog of lies that the jury had been exposed to was fast fading. The prosecution was turning a good deed into an admission of guilt. She was making him out to be a liar, when in fact he was the only one who had told the truth. By the time she began her next question he was so agitated that he had to ask her to repeat it.

"I said, is it reasonable to expect the court to believe you would take risks like that for the sake of an ex-friend who had, as you tell it, just hoodwinked you into tagging along on a killing for no other reason than because he thought you might enjoy the show?"

Ira objected, but the judge overruled him.

"Isn't what really happened is that you yourself killed Andrew Mott because you thought he was someone who had sold you bad drugs, and then asked Tommy McCready to drive you to Prospect Park where you took the same gun you had just used to murder Mr. Mott and buried it?"

"No, it's not."

"Isn't it also true, Mr. Conover, that it was your own idea to make the stop on Flatbush Avenue and to confront the group of young black men you saw assembled there? And that it was you, not anyone else, who then got out of the car and shot Mr. Mott in cold blood in full view of everyone in the car as well as Mr. Mott's friends?"

"No, it's not. I didn't kill nobody. It's a fucking lie!"

The judge called the witness to order and warned him there would be no further use of profane language in her courtroom. But Billy scarcely heard her. A steam engine seemed to be roaring through his head. He instinctively reached into his pocket to see what relief he might find there. But his freshly pressed suit was empty.

"I have no more questions of this witness, Your Honor. But I would like to call Brendan McCauley at this time to the stand."

Ira was on his feet objecting. The judge asked both attorneys to approach the bench for a conference. Billy watched anxiously while they whispered among themselves for the better part of a minute. Then the judge told Brendan to step forward.

"She can't do this," Billy said to his lawyer. "It's against the Rules of Procedure."

"She claims she couldn't locate him until this morning. That sounds like a crock to me. I told the judge I'm filing for a mistrial, but there's nothing I can do in the meantime. It's her courtroom."

Billy watched Brendan walk slowly toward the witness box. He was dressed in a clean pair of chinos and an open-neck sport shirt. Billy knew he didn't own a suit. Brendan sat down, then was asked to rise again to be sworn in. When he raised his right hand he stared at the back of the courtroom as if he were at a military review.

Seated again, he suddenly didn't know where to look. His eyes glanced off Billy's for a fraction of a second before finding a safe resting place on the back wall. He stated his name, address and employment—building manager.

"Mr. McCauley, how long have you known the accused, William Conover?"

The harmlessness of the question seemed to surprise Brendan. He looked Billy's way before answering.

"I know him fifteen years, maybe a little longer."

"You attended elementary and high school together? And you live just a few doors from where he and his family live, is that correct?"

"That's right."

"Mr. McCauley, on the morning of March 29th, did Billy Conover pay you a visit at your apartment?"

"March 29th? Was that the morning after the yam was wasted?"

The ADA hung her head, waiting for the inevitable caution from the judge.

"There will be no racial slurs permitted in this courtroom, young man."

Brendan regarded her with confusion, not realizing he had said anything wrong.

The prosecutor continued.

"March 29th was the day after the killing of Andrew Mott."

"Right," Brendan said, his acne glowing pink. Billy noted he had nicked some of his pimples shaving. "Yeah, I saw Billy that morning."

Billy could imagine the funk his old friend must be in and wondered if he had helped himself to a few cc's of smack to ease the way. But he realized, no however the trial turned out, that he wouldn't change places with Brendan McCauley for all the dope in Brownsville.

"Did you and he have a conversation?"

"Conversation?"

"Did you speak with one another?"

"Sure, we spoke."

"Would you please tell the court what it was you discussed?"

This was obviously what Brendan had been brought here to say, and he knew it. But he looked as if he had just been tied to a spit and someone was stoking a fire beneath.

"Well, he said...that if anybody asked where he was the night before..."

"That would be the night of the 28th."

Brendan regarded her mutely for a moment, then continued, "He said that if anybody asked where he was that night, I should say he was there with me."

"That he had been in your apartment throughout the evening and night?"

"Yeah."

"Had he in fact been there with you?"

Brendan shook his head.

"Please answer out loud," the judge instructed.

Brendan lifted his head halfway and said, "No, he wasn't."

The ADA turned and walked over to the prosecutor's table, glanced at a note and said, "That's all, Your Honor."

The judge asked if the defense had any questions for this witness. Ira said he did.

"Mr. McCauley, you say that you and Billy have been good friends for some time, is that right?"

"That's right," Brendan said, looking more at ease with Billy's lawyer than he had with the State's.

"What sort of things did you do together—as friends, I mean?"

Brendan stared down at the metal bar surrounding the witness box and drew the corners of his mouth down sharply.

"I dunno. Hang out."

"Watch TV? Play cards?"

"Yeah, stuff like that."

"How about paying visits to your neighbor's houses and stealing their money and jewelry?"

The prosecutor jumped to her feet.

"Your Honor, this witness is not on trial."

The judge turned toward the Legal Aid attorney.

"Mr. Greenberg, please confine yourself to matters that are directly relevant to this case."

"I'm trying to establish, Your Honor, that this witness and my client engaged in criminal activity together and that the witness may therefore have been induced to testify in return for a consideration by the State."

The judge frowned, not wanting to give further cause for a mistrial. Finally she said, "You may proceed, but be very careful, Mr. Greenberg."

"Mr. McCauley, were not you and Billy Conover partners in crime?"

Blushing so brightly his acne looked like little volcanoes, Brendan said, "Naw, we didn't do nothing like that."

"Isn't it true, Mr. McCauley, that you yourself selected targets to be hit and then directed how the burglaries would be carried out?"

Brendan laughed nervously. "Naw, not me."

"And isn't it also true that you have been promised freedom from prosecution for those offenses if you testify today against my client?"

Brendan looked as if he might choke but managed to get out, "Naw. No way."

"I have no more questions of this...witness, Your Honor."


"How did you know what Brendan and me was up to?" Billy asked in amazement when Ira returned to the table.

"Sixth sense," Ira said, looking oddly downhearted.

"What happens now?"

"Summations."

"Already?"

Ira turned toward his client and asked, "Is there anything you want me to say to the DA before we begin?"

"You mean about copping a plea?"

"Not that the judge is likely to accept one at this late date."

Billy hesitated only a second before shaking his head vigorously. "I'll take my chances."

The summations were shorter and less passionate than Billy had expected after all the hours of TV dramas he had watched. Taking short mincing steps in front of the jury box, the ADA argued that the preponderance of evidence—the occupants of the car who testified that Billy committed the murder plus Billy's own admission that he buried the murder weapon with his own hands and then sought to elude the police—proved he was guilty.

Ira maintained in a firm but scarcely audible drone that his client had no believable motive for the slaying, nor any history of violence and was the victim of a conspiracy to acquit the real murderer who would walk out of the courtroom free, thanks to intimidation of the witnesses by the police, the prosecution and the friends of the killer.

Throughout the summations the jurors regarded the two diminutive lawyers with what seemed to Billy more curiosity than attention, as if they were rather clever monkeys who were part of an experiment to see how much of the legal profession could be taken over by apes. When they were finsihed the judge charged the jury and they retired to decide Billy's fate.

He had not been able to guess from any of the jurors' faces if they believed him innocent. The stout black women showed no anger or any other emotion when the prosecution described the brutal murder of Andrew Mott. Skepticism, in fact, seemed to be the prevailing emotion among all jury members.

He was given a sandwich and a cup of coffee, but he had no appetite. He was surprised to see the other occupants of the holding pen scarfing down their food. One even asked for Billy's sandwich if he wasn't going to eat it. At what seemed the beginning of his third hour in the pen he asked a guard for the time and was amazed to find that scarcely an hour had passed.

The smell of human flesh filled the cell. This or something worse would be his fate for the next twenty-five years if the jury found him guilty. He had asked Ira how long he thought deliberations might take, but the lawyer only shrugged and said, "Two hours...two days."

He sipped cold coffee and considered offering up a prayer. He hadn't prayed in years—not officially. From time to time, when he was in a tight spot rifling through somebody's pants pockets and heard them stir in their sleep, he begged God to save his skin, promising he would give up his life of crime and look for an honest job first thing in the morning. But then his hapless victim would roll over and go back to sleep and the promise he had made to the deity would be forgotten.

By what right did he have to ask God for anything? If God wasn't worth praying to all the years he had flaunted His commandments, why should He listen today?

"I don't give a shit about myself," he prayed nevertheless. "I guess I deserve what I get. But the kid didn't ask to have no criminal for a father or a whore for a mother. Don't let him end up like I did. Don't let him grow up with no father and not giving a shit about himself."

"Five'll get you ten you're thinking about a piece of ass," a familiar voice replied.

Billy found his cellmate standing over him.

"What the hell're you doing here?"

"Motion hearing. Some bullshit. But it's okay with me as long as I get out of the cell for a while. How's your case going?"

"The jury's still out."

"You must be shitting a brick."

"Say, man," a thin Latino at the other end of the bench interrupted, "Your lawyer name of Sharkey?"

"Naw," Billy said. "Greenberg. Ira Greenberg."

"The reason I ask, I hear Sharkey's supposed to be on the up. Greenberg's probably cool too. He sounds Jewish."

"Conover?" Billy heard the guard call as his cellmate was beginning to describe how he had imprisoned a young girl in a tree house.

"See you later," the man said as the guard led Billy away.

The courtroom had the enervated, after-lunch atmosphere of a classroom waiting for a boring teacher to show up. Billy's mother and sister were seated in their usual places and gave brave smiles. Rosemary was sitting behind them, wearing a dress. She gave him a little wave.

"All rise."

The judge carefully arranged her long robes, then asked if the jury had reached a verdict. A short elderly black man declared they had, and a court officer received a slip of paper from him and carried it to the judge. She studied it for several seconds, then looked down at the jury box and asked the foreman to read their decision.

The court officer called out the first charge: Murder in the Second Degree.

"How do you find the defendant?"

"We find the defendant," the man said, his voice suddenly going hoarse so that he had to clear it with a bark which startled his expectant audience, "not guilty."

Billy's knees began to shake. He felt a hand grip his shoulder. It was a powerful hold, like that of someone trying to save a drowning man.

"And the second charge: Reckless Endangerment?"

The old man cleared his throat dramatically and squared off his shoulders. Billy realized the foreman was about the same age his father would have been had he lived.

"We find the defendant...guilty as charged."

Billy winced.

"How could they find me guilty? How could they fucking find me guilty?"

Ira hushed him. "Easy, Billy. We beat the big one."

"Sentencing will be in this courtroom at 10:00 a.m. tomorrow morning."

# CHAPTER TWENTY-FOUR

The next morning Ira pointed out that his client had never before been charged with a violent crime nor even with so much as carrying a knife. The prosecution reminded the judge that the defendant never denied being present at the murder of Andrew Mott and only cooperated with the authorities under considerable pressure.

The judge asked Billy if he had anything to say before she passed sentencing. He said he did.

He stood up and made an effort to lift his chin higher than he was accustomed to holding it. There was no sign of sympathy, retribution or any other emotion on the judge's face. He wondered if she had a son of her own and if he were the same age Andrew Mott would have been.

Then he began to speak, without rehearsal, just thinking out loud as he had been doing all the previous night as he lay in his cell, trying to understand how he had ended up in this mess. His cellmate had gotten released on bail, so Billy had had plenty of quiet time to mull things over. As he listened to the sounds of the prison—the distant voices of guards, inmates calling out in their sleep, a hard rain that seemed to demand thunder and lightening but got none—he waited for some meaning, some defining pattern to illuminate what had happened to him, the way visions of truth came to the saints of his youth. But none occurred, just the senseless noise of grown men dreaming the dreams of frightened children and the hard footfalls of their keepers.

He had tried again to pray, for guidance this time, but found the well of his faith bone dry. He didn't feel any special remorse on that account. If anything, he felt ashamed for trying to pray at all, crying out for help like a scared child, when the only one who could do him any good was himself

What most frightened him was not the loss of freedom he faced or even the possibility of violence in some upstate prison manned by local yokels. It was confinement itself, a kind of darkness even when the lights were on. How would he endure that for months on end with no supply of drugs to ease the anguish? He wasn't even eligible for methadone maintenance.

It was only shortly before dawn that he finally dropped into a light, uneasy sleep. He dreamed he was a kid again. He and his father were back on that same beach in the Rockaways. His father seemed remarkably young, but then Billy realized the man's youth was more a perception of the son's own maturing years rather than of the man's ability to cheat time. They were playing catch near the lapping remains of breakers crashing nearby. With a dream's convenience of allowing him to be both child and adult at the same, he found himself filled with gratitude for the man's return from the dead or from a close call with death, it wasn't clear which. But whether resurrection or miraculous recovery, the father who had abandoned him for so long was back, and the force of the love he felt for the man was shocking. Where did it come from? How could he have managed to hide it from himself all these years? The sky over the ocean began to darken with the approach of sunset. But he felt none of the instinctive fear he ordinarily felt at the close of day.

A boat's horn sounded and he awoke to morning reveille in the jail. He tried to hold onto the image of his father, so convincing even when he tested it against the ordinary standards of what was and was not real. The image faded as the sounds of the prison filled his consciousness, but his father's presence persisted on some deeper, less conscious level. It was as if he had been afforded an actual visit with the man, just as the characters in epics and the Bible were visited in dreams by gods or messengers of Yahweh. And even though no words were spoken between him and his father, the long indictment he had held against the man for leaving him was now lifted and he knew he would no longer feel abandoned in the same way again.

He kept his head raised and told the judge he had been stupid to get into Tommy McCready's car that night. He also said he had been wasting his life, hanging out with people who'll only end up in jail themselves or OD. Then he added in a voice that caused even the prosecution attorney to look up from her notes and listen.

"Your Honor, I deserve to get the maximum, just for stupidity," he said, as his own lawyer glanced at the judge in alarm. "But I want you to know I'm very sorry about what happened to Mr. Mott, even though I didn't shoot him myself and I never intended him no harm."

"I know that won't bring Mr. Mott back to life, and it sure as hell won't make his mother feel any better. But I mean it, and I want to say I don't mind going to jail now, because I deserve to be punished for my part in what happened.

"That's all I have to say. Thank you for listening, Your Honor."

The judge glanced down at some papers in front of her, although to everyone in the courtroom it was evident she was buying time to collect her thoughts. Billy's mother was weeping quietly, as were Cathleen and Rosemary. A middle-aged black woman in the front row sat dry-eyed, staring into the middle distance.

Finally the judge spoke.

"Before I pass sentence, can the prosecution tell me if steps are being taken to bring charges against anyone else in the matter of the murder of Andrew Mott?"

Surprised by this unusual aside, the ADA stepped forward hesitantly and cleared her throat.

"Your Honor, we're looking into that matter, yes."

The judge scowled at the pre-sentencing report in front of her, then said quietly, "I certainly hope so."

Then, to Billy she said: "Mr. Conover, you speak persuasively. And your record indeed does not show any arrests for violent crimes. However, the nature of this case is such," she said, at first not looking at the defendant but then, as if having to choose judicial duty over personal sentiments, confronting him directly, "that a young man lost his life as the result of a brutal and vicious murder to which, as you have yourself admitted, you were at the very least an uncaring bystander. I appreciate the remorse you just expressed, but remorse cannot bring the dead back to life, nor change in any way what happened that night.

"I therefore sentence you to a maximum of three years in the state penitentiary at Dannemora."

For a moment, Billy stood silent and unmoving. But then he said without any trace of sarcasm, "Thank you, Your Honor."

The court officers approached to escort him from the courtroom. He hurriedly thanked his lawyer who embraced him warmly. As he was led away, he blew a kiss to his mother and sister and gave the thumbs-up sign to Rosemary.

Then he was led out of the courtroom.

www.ingramcontent.com/pod-product-compliance
Lightning Source LLC
Chambersburg PA
CBHW050533260626
47157CB00004B/1591